SECRETLY

TRANSFORMATION SERIES
BOOK 2

TALYA BLAINE

Ebook ISBN: 978-1-959336-01-3

Paperback ISBN: 978-1-959336-04-4

CONTENTS

1

DESSERT

The private elevator let Quinn off in the center of the light, airy landing. A gleaming gray floor and soaring windows encircled the three hundred sixty-degree entry to Jonathan's penthouse. Across from the elevator the sweeping gallery narrowed, forming a generous hallway into his apartment, no front door required.

The scent of coconut and sautéing garlic drew her in. A shimmer of anticipation fluttered as she slipped off her ballet flats and left them under the steel console table. Minimalist and masculine.

It's just dinner.

No reason to feel butterflies. They were friends; they would no doubt enjoy each other's company over a home-cooked meal. Good conversation, his dry, self-deprecating sense of humor, the kind, easy-going way he had about him.

Nothing was going to happen tonight. To ensure it, she had not shaved her legs. At least not higher than the spot by her ankle where the hem of her white jeans hit.

Partial-leg stubble, for some strange reason, seemed

worse than whole-leg stubble, and it offered added insurance. Nothing was going to happen.

The painted concrete floor was cool against her bare feet. "Come right in when you get here—we'll find each other," he had texted with a winking emoji just as her train left the eastern Long Island station a couple of hours ago.

The apartment was quiet except for noise from the kitchen—the click-click-click of a gas burner igniting, a lid clanging against a pot, the seal of the refrigerator door breaking as he opened it.

Her mind flashed back to their time on the movie set, how he always seemed surrounded by noise. You could hear the TV or music coming from his trailer, even when he wasn't there. Her impression at the time was that he didn't like being alone.

"Hellooo," she called.

"Hey." From the warmth in that one word, she could already picture the sparkle in his eyes, the crinkled skin at their corners when he smiled. "In here."

"Mmm, I'll just follow the wonderful smells." The scent of chili peppers tickled her nostrils. The startup of the exhaust fan drowned out the crackle of hot oil.

In the kitchen, he was standing by the stove, a wide gas range with double ovens—it was obvious he loved to cook. He held a whisk in one hand and the rim of a hammered copper mixing bowl against his white apron in the other.

The light blue button-down shirt set off the warm brown of his eyes. The sleeves were rolled, revealing the curls on his forearms, his jeans faded in all the right places, she just happened to notice once he put down the bowl, took off the apron, and came around the island to give her a quick—regrettably quick—hug.

He gestured to a stool in front of the granite countertop. "Have a seat. Can I get you a glass of wine?"

"Please." She sat facing the monster stove while he uncorked a sweating bottle of white and poured her a glass.

A second later the oven timer beeped, and he hurried to tend to it. As she took a sip of the peppery wine, she watched him work. Capable, confident. His placid expression fit a man at home in his kitchen.

"So this is what you do in the daylight hours," she teased, an unplanned note of flirtation sneaking in.

His laugh was rich, an instant reward.

The skin around his eyes bunched with his smile, and he looked at her without lifting his head. A shiver snaked its way down her body.

He raised a finger to signal he had to take care of one more thing. A few deft movements that she couldn't see at the range, and he turned toward her, wiping his hands on the apron on the counter. "This needs to simmer a few minutes. Let's get out of here."

He picked up his half-full glass from the island and gestured toward the French doors at the other side of the open living area.

On the way out, she left her purse on the coffee table in front of the sofa. Running the length of the opposite wall was a long bookshelf that stretched all the way to the high ceiling. A wooden library ladder leaned against an upper shelf. She quickly scanned his collection of books: shelf after shelf of travel guides, art history, politics, world history, cookbooks, fiction.

And then her eyes landed on a section of familiar spines. The typography, the progression in hue from one to the next told her he owned all of her books.

Except for the last one, which she too lacked.

He must have read her mind. "I'm eagerly awaiting the next one."

A sinking feeling tugged in her chest. "I'm afraid it might be a long wait. I'm officially on hiatus." Officially, at least as far as she was concerned.

"No. Why?"

She turned and looked up at him. "I still haven't been able to write anything."

"That's understandable. Won't Devon work with you on the deadline?"

"They have already. I mean, I really haven't been able to come up with anything that feels worth writing about. But . . . can we not go there tonight?"

"We don't have to."

"I don't mean to shut you down. It's just that some things I feel ready to tackle and others, not so much yet." *Like you.*

In the month since she told Leigh she would not deliver a next book, she had not once regretted her decision. Yes, sometimes she missed writing, but if she were honest, what she felt more was guilt.

Guilt that she was shirking obligation, guilt that she *should* write rather than that she was driven to it, like she used to be, the scenes in her mind compelling her to tell the story, to capture it in words.

"I asked Leigh to figure out how to cancel the publishing contract. I'll give back the money. It's just,"—she touched her chest—"there's nothing there, you know?"

"I understand, I do. And when the time's right, you'll come back to it. I'm confident of that—you're an amazing writer." He gave her shoulder a quick, supportive squeeze. "So, what's in the ready-to-tackle category?"

"Okay, maybe 'ready' was ambitious." She rubbed the warm hand on her shoulder. "But I do have news."

"Oh? Tell me."

"I'm moving. In two weeks."

"Wow. That's big." Concern flashed across his face. "You said you were thinking of selling, but that's like lightning fast."

"Right? Crazy-fast. I called a neighbor who's a real estate agent to talk about the process. Turns out a colleague in her office had a client looking in the area but couldn't find what they wanted. I'm not exaggerating—within twenty-four hours of seeing the house, they made an offer, above where we would have priced it. The only catch is, I have to be out before I close on the new place."

"Where's the new place?" He rubbed the back of his neck like he was expecting the answer to be bad.

"I found this small restored farmhouse in the Hudson Valley. Like I told Leigh, I'll still be close enough for regular lunches." Noting the worry in his eyes, she added, "and dinners. I'm trying to see the fact that it's happening so quickly as a good sign. It also lowers the risk of cold feet."

His eyes narrowed, assessing. "*Do* you have cold feet?"

"Moving is the right thing, money-wise and memory-wise. And the new place is adorable. You'll have to see it."

"I want to." As they reached the wall of floor-to-ceiling glass, he opened one of the two sets of doors and gestured for her to go first, onto the expansive, sunny terrace in the sky.

Together, they walked to the railing and set their drinks on the narrow wood balustrade. For a few silent moments, they stood side by side at the waist-high glass, looking out over the unobstructed view of the city.

Standing here next to him reminded her of the night of Leigh's well-intended invasion, the night the two of them stood at her kitchen window and looked out toward the dark ocean.

It was easy for them to be quiet together.

"The faster I move out," she continued without turning to face him, "the faster new people can enjoy it like we did." She shrugged a shoulder. "At least that's the positive spin I'm putting on it."

He nodded, lifting his wineglass to take a sip. "It's a great house."

"It is. It was." A twinge of sadness nudged her to change the subject. "*You* have a great place. This view is incredible. It feels like a different world up here."

He chuckled, but those deep brown eyes dimmed. "It does feel that way sometimes."

"What do you mean? Removed? Isolated?"

He nodded. *Lonely*, she realized. His gaze moved back to the city stretched out before them, and she didn't press.

He turned toward her again as if he were about to say more, but the cooking timer beeped faintly from inside. "Have a seat." He gestured to the rattan sectional. A tray on the table in front of it held two stacked bowls and shiny silverware rolled in cloth napkins. "You can set the table." The sparkle came back to his eyes when he smiled. "Be right back."

A few minutes later, he returned carrying another tray and set it down. In one ceramic bowl was fluffy, steaming white rice. When he took the lid off the other, the aroma of seafood and cilantro filled the evening air. She used to love seafood. "It smells *fantastic*."

"Hungry?"

"I am now." Food had been an afterthought the past fifteen months, something she considered mostly when dizziness struck or her stomach gurgled. Nothing tasted like it used to. Flavors had lost their vibrancy, reduced to black and white.

He topped off their wineglasses and sat down next to her, spooned rice into their bowls, and bathed it with a ladleful of creamy stew studded with pink shrimp and bright green herbs.

"It's *moqueca de camarão*. It'll be in the upcoming Brazil episode. *Bom proveito*. Enjoy."

"*Bom proveito*," she repeated, scooping both rice and stew onto her spoon. The flavors exploded in her mouth. "It *tastes* fantastic."

He took a bite slowly and evaluated. "You like it?"

Her taste buds sprung to life, along with her appetite. "I do. The lime, coconut, the heat . . . it's a perfect mix."

She pictured him learning how to make the dish on his trip. He would accompany the person hosting him as they shopped in a tropical market, then chopped cilantro or deveined shrimp and prepared the meal in his local host's home kitchen. "When's the episode going to air?"

"Next week. Why, are you planning to watch?" His smile was playful.

"I might. If I'm not too busy with, you know, very important things," she played back. "I know the host."

"I'm sorry." He wrinkled his brow, feigning concern. "I've heard he can be an ass."

"Don't believe everything you hear. Besides, I like to form my own opinions."

He patted her knee, two platonic pats, although she still felt the tingling charge along her skin through the napkin and her jeans.

They ate slowly and talked, and after a while both of them filled their bowls with a second helping. Finally she sat back, unable to eat another bite, and he piled their dishes onto the tray.

She reached for it to carry inside. "Please, let me help."

"I've got it," he said. "Sit and relax."

As the low evening sun blazed hot from the west, rain clouds drifted from the south. He looked at the sky. "Actually, why don't you come inside and have a seat on the couch while I call the producers to lodge a complaint—I specifically asked them to arrange nice weather for tonight, but it looks like it might rain."

She giggled and noticed his chest rise and fall, a quick breath. Had he felt butterflies about tonight, like she had?

She followed him in and sat on the sofa, modern but comfortable, while he worked in the kitchen. "Are you sure I can't do anything?" She hated feeling useless.

He looked up at her across the space. "I'm sure. You're buying and selling real estate—you should take every opportunity to relax while you can."

A few minutes later, silverware clinked as he came toward her with the tray again. This time it held a small, red enamel pot, its wooden knob partially covered with a dishtowel. "Dessert's a surprise. Close your eyes."

The thought that immediately popped to mind, she should not have had it. *What if I don't? Will you blindfold me?*

SHE LISTENED as he set the tray on the coffee table. The couch cushion shifted as he sat down next to her, his knee grazing hers. She heard the lid clang against the pot and pictured his large hand on the small knob, removing it.

"Keep your eyes closed." He tapped her lips once,

quickly, with his finger. "Open." When she complied, he placed a spoonful of warm liquid on her tongue. "What do you taste?"

The earthy, smoky scent of chocolate teased her nose as the tepid liquid, almost as thick as honey, coated her tongue. She swirled it around to really taste it and swallowed.

The warmth continued to spread, although the lush, bitter, sweet liquid—some kind of creamy, hot chocolate drink?—was no longer in her mouth. "Cayenne?" she asked. "Also cream? Vanilla?" And there was something else she couldn't identify.

"Close your eyes," he said gruffly. She hadn't realized she had opened them. "You're on the right track, so I'll give you another chance. First, here, hold this."

He put the dishtowel in her hand, which he brought to her face, in front of her eyes. The fabric was warm from the heat of the pot. "You didn't follow the rules."

So he *was* going to blindfold her.

Arousal tingled low in her belly, lower than it should tingle with friends.

He tied the cloth around the back of her head while his breath rustled the hair on her neck. She felt him sit beside her again, and then he pulled the fabric down until the light was gone.

The lid clanked against the rim of the pot once more as his weight shifted from the edge of the couch near the coffee table back toward her. "Open again . . . oh, shit. Some dripped. Hold on—I'll get a paper towel."

The sound of his footsteps moved in the direction of the kitchen, and she heard the rip of paper towel and the trickle of water against the metal sink.

More footsteps and soon he was beside her again.

Gentle tugging at the bottom of her blouse told her he must have taken ahold of the hem to blot it.

"Hmm, that's not doing a whole lot," he said. "We can soak it with some stain remover in the sink." She could feel his hands on the fabric on each side near her waist. "Can I take it off?"

"Sure."

Undress me.

His fingers grazed the skin on her side as he started to lift her top, sending a shiver through the rest of her.

"Hey. Did you really spill, or is this a ploy?" she teased.

His laugh touched off another shiver. Incredible how her body reacted to him.

"Give me your hand." He guided her index finger to a wet spot on the fabric. "See? No ploy."

He let go of her hand and lifted off the blouse, his knuckles skimming the length of her sides. Listening to the way his breath hitched, then slowed, the hot chocolate stain would not be the only wet spot.

She crossed her arms and breathed in deeply to slow her racing pulse as she heard him remove the pot lid again.

"One more quick taste, and then I'll get you something to wear." He blew to cool what she assumed was another spoonful of molten chocolate. "Open."

She did as instructed. Nothing happened, except he swallowed and whispered, "On second thought."

A drop of heat landed on her chest. Then another and another, not far from the edge of the lace cups of her bra.

"What are you . . ." Oh, goodness. His mouth was on her skin, licking and softly sucking where the chocolate had fallen. ". . . doing?"

"I'm tasting," he drawled, his words soft against her skin before he moved away. "Is that okay?"

She brought her hand to his shoulder. "It's okay. But nothing's changed from what we said in the hospital . . . I'm not ready for us, this, to be a re—"

"I know. Not a relationship. But I'm perfectly willing to be used again."

She laughed at that and stroked the side of his neck, his jawline, with her thumb. "We said we were going to take a step back, get to know each other better."

"Mm-hm," he uttered, breath against skin. "That is *exactly* what I'm doing. I'm learning quite a lot, in fact."

"What are you learning?" she managed to ask.

The pot lid clinked again a couple of times and she held her breath.

This time, he didn't blow as long. The hot drops landed inside the edge of her bra, at the curve of her breast. They reminded her of the molten wax at Octavia's. Only there, the sensation, the heat, was confined to her back. With Jonathan, with his mouth on her, with his fingers holding the lacy triangle of fabric away from her skin, it spread like wildfire, warming her everywhere.

Ev-er-y-where.

His mouth moved over her breast to the sensitive skin of her areola while his tongue swirled and sucked her nipple.

"I'm learning that you like this"—his teeth scraped her pebbled skin—"and that when I do this"—his fingertips lightly caressed her belly, her ribcage, the side of her back—"you arch toward me."

He pressed her closer as if to illustrate. "And your breathing gets heavier," he whispered into her ear, sending a flutter down her neck.

The strokes of his hand and his tongue slowed, and he pulled back from her body. "But you're right. I heard what you said in the hospital, and I don't want to push you."

He lifted the bottom of the dishtowel, and she found his eyes riveted to her—dark, magnetic and, although she wished otherwise, caring. "I'm sorry," he said. "I shouldn't have started that. Let's stop."

She leaned closer, her hand around the back of his neck, and rested her forehead against his lips. He pressed his mouth to her skin but did not kiss her.

"Don't stop," she panted. "You're not pushing me. I don't want you to stop."

HOLDING HER FACE, he pulled back. "If you're sure, then I won't."

"I'm sure."

He slid off the couch to kneel in front of her before he pulled the makeshift blindfold down over her eyes again.

He had not planned on this. Tonight was supposed to be a casual, platonic dinner between friends, a chance to catch up on the past few weeks and to learn more about each other after their mostly silent rendezvous.

Take things slow, not rush into dating.

He brought his mouth to her breast once more and swirled his tongue lazily around her nipple, laving and sucking. He could take *this* as slowly as she wanted. For as long as she would let him.

In the past, he might—might—have thought to blindfold her with the dishtowel when she opened her eyes earlier, but he would not have thought to drip chocolate on her.

He had not been that imaginative before her.

But seeing her eyes covered reminded him of their nights together, including the one when she was bound and blindfolded while he dripped a melting ice cube on her breasts.

She had writhed against the restraints, her hips rocking back and forth. And then he remembered how he had found her at Octavia's dungeon a few weeks ago, the trails of wax crisscrossing her back. Why not chocolate, food of the gods?

She was beautiful and sensual, and his cock grew harder against his jeans just looking at her flushed cheeks, at how her lips outlined her partially open mouth, at how his mouth on her breasts brought her pleasure.

He leaned back on his heels and twisted around to remove the pot lid and grab the spoon again.

But this time, he thought better of that and instead dipped his index and middle fingers into the still-warm liquid. With his other hand cupped underneath, he brought his fingers to her mouth and wet her parted lips, then her tongue, with chocolate.

She licked her lips and closed her mouth around his fingers. Her tongue twined around them, tasting it, tasting him.

Drops of pre-cum oozed from his shaft as he imagined it in place of his fingers.

"What's the verdict?" he asked, "the secret ingredient."

"I can't think right now. Tell me."

He couldn't think much either with her sucking his fingers. "Cardamom. It's hot chocolate, *chocolat chaud*, with cayenne and cardamom."

When she had licked them clean, he took his fingers from her mouth, brushed her cheek with his thumb, traced her jaw, reached his hand around her neck. Her chin tilted upward, as if she were leaning in, wondering what he was going to do next. He caressed the back of her head, combed his fingers through her hair, and without thinking, moved closer to kiss her.

At the touch of their lips, she froze and her breath caught, jarring him with realization.

He had almost crossed a line; her old rules were still in force. "I forgot," he blurted, and stroked her cheek. "I forgot."

"It's just that . . ." she stammered.

He did not want to hear the "just friends" spiel again.

He got it—they could fool around as long as they weren't romantically involved, as long as he didn't expect anything more. "Shh," he murmured with his finger on her lips, like she had done with him that first night. "I forgot. I'm sorry. It won't happen again."

He kept his finger there for a few seconds, until the tension in her jaw loosened and she relaxed against the sofa cushion. Still kneeling in front of her, he stroked her long stretch of belly with his fingertips, from the underwire of her bra to the waistband of her white jeans. Up and down he trailed, as the patterns of goose bumps on her skin changed with each light caress and her lips parted, expelling the quietest, sexiest moan.

The next time his hand was near her waistband, he shifted direction and caressed side to side, just underneath the soft denim.

When she made that noise again, he undid the metal button and took hold of the tab of her zipper but waited to pull it down. "Is this okay?"

At the sound of her yes and the uneven breaths that followed, he brought his hands around those fucking beautiful hips to her ass, so he could slide the jeans down her legs.

She lifted her pelvis in cooperation. As the denim

bunched by her ankles, she lifted her feet one by one to push it off.

He wanted to sit back and simply watch her, to tease her with anticipation and see how she would react, but he also didn't want to wait. With one hand, he moved the fabric of her matching lace panties to the side and, with the other, slid his finger along her folds, swollen and wet.

Damn, he had missed this, missed her. But he did not say it.

Another quiet moan escaped her parted lips, and she arched her hips while he continued. Back and forth many times before sliding one finger and then another into her. He pushed deeper, stroked inside her, retreated and pressed deep again.

She pitched her hips in time with his movements, a soft moan riding each breath out. Without stopping, he let go of her panties so he could undo his pants.

Thank you well-worn Levi's for the button-fly he could yank open with one hand.

He was so hard his cock sprang from the slit of his boxers, sticky with pre-cum. He stroked himself while keeping up his rhythm inside her with his other hand.

As he caressed and pressed and circled her sensitive inner mound, her head tipped back and she cried out, grabbing his forearm. The movement of her hips hastened and soon she was clutching and releasing his soaked fingers.

He slowed but kept moving inside her while she came apart, feeling the muscles of her core tighten, watching her lips move in pleasure, watching his other hand working those last few strokes. And while her contractions and sighs slowed, he watched his load douse her belly.

He waited until she stopped clenching and slowly, lightly, resumed stroking her G-spot. She gasped and grabbed his arm again, and he knew what it meant. *Too much.*

He stayed still, then gradually withdrew his fingers, the pads white and wrinkled as if he'd taken a long, hot shower. He brought one to her mouth like he had with the chocolate.

"Taste yourself," he rasped, and she did. He saved the second for himself.

A rivulet of semen dripped toward her panties, and his limp dick ticked as he watched it seep into the lace. He swiped the same two fingers through it and brought them to her mouth again. "Taste this." As she had done with the chocolate, she sucked them clean.

He reached for the box of tissues on the side table when her phone rang from inside her purse.

"Do you want to answer it?" He lifted the towel away from her eyes.

"No. They'll leave a voice mail."

A second later, it sounded again. He looked at her, and she shook her head, now resting against the back of the couch. *No.*

As he finished cleaning her sticky belly and his dick, it rang, chimed, and buzzed several more times.

"Alright, alright," she said, winded from their intensity or from frustration, he wasn't sure. "Can you give it to me, please?"

She took the phone from him and looked at the screen. "It was Leigh." Their mutual friend; her agent. The text Quinn showed him read, "PICK UP!!!!!!!!!!"

It rang again, and she answered. "What's going *on?* Are you okay?"

He could hear Leigh's agitation, although he couldn't

make out what she was saying. All he knew was that Quinn's brow furrowed and her eyes widened.

"*No.* It's only a few weeks away. They can't do that."

More mile-a-minute staccato from Leigh's end.

"Calm down," Quinn said. "There has to be a solution; we'll figure it out." She ran her hand through her hair and waved it back off her shoulder, ready for business. Leigh continued with what sounded like a tirade.

"Let me call you back in a little while when I'm home." Quinn gazed at her bare feet, avoiding looking at him although he was sitting on the floor right beside them.

He heard Leigh make a long sound—something like, "Ohhhh"—and then, "date night."

So Quinn must have told her they were having dinner tonight. That she hadn't kept it a secret, he took as a baby step, a positive one.

Quinn crossed the arm that wasn't holding the phone over her chest. "She can't see you," he whispered, and wrapped his hands around her calves to stroke the skin at the back of each knee.

If it didn't sound so serious, he would tease her more and stroke somewhere else. As it was, she swatted him away and put her arm back over her breasts.

Leigh raised her voice. "Is he right there? Jonathan, can you . . .?"

"Hanging up now," Quinn said. "Call you back."

She tapped the screen and set the phone on the table before leaning back into the cushions and letting out a huge sigh.

"Dare I ask?"

"Becca's building had a water line break. There's a lot of flooding. She just got to Leigh's place—she's staying there for who knows how long. And the restaurant on the first floor, where she and Charles were going to have the wedding *canceled*. Two hundred eighty people. Bride-to-be and mother are both totally freaking out."

"I never heard of anything like that." Not that he was up on wedding stuff. He and Delphine had had a small ceremony with her immediate family at their vineyard and a casual luncheon, which stretched across the afternoon into dinner. One long, jovial outdoor table on a blindingly sunny day—vases full of freshly cut wildflowers, platters of food her aunts and grandmother had spent days preparing, undulating hills of heirloom grapevines framing the scene.

The familiar wave of guilt rose, and he stuffed it away.

"Me either. With fifty people, okay, you could find *some* restaurant, or squeeze everyone into Leigh's apartment, but two hundred eighty? On short notice? In New York City? Not a lot of options."

"No. You should probably get going so you can call her back before she melts down completely. I'm not kicking you out—you're welcome to stay—but now you have a good excuse."

He squeezed the top of her knee and stood up, helping her to her feet.

"Yeah, I need to go." She glanced around for her jeans, but he took her arms and turned her to face him.

Touching his chest, she slowly smoothed his shirt near the pocket. Evidently, she could tell what he was thinking. "I'm not sorry about tonight," she added, "but I do need to leave."

"And if Leigh and Becca weren't in crisis mode?"

Why did he just ask her that?

It made him sound needy, not to mention dumb, like he wasn't comprehending what she had already told him several times.

"I'd still be going home tonight. You know that." Her gaze descended from his eyes to his lips and his chest, and her hand encircled the side of his neck before she moved it away. "Even though I don't really want to."

He nodded. At least she was talking. At least she was direct about what they were and were not doing and about how she felt conflicted. Although he already gleaned that from the way she looked at him and touched him. "I understand. I'll grab you a shirt to wear home."

In his closet he found his smallest shirt, a button-down that would still hang big on her but that she could tuck in or tie in front like he'd seen some women do.

Also in the plus column, it would be large and comfortable enough for her to wear to bed. He would love to see her wake up in it some morning, wrinkled from sleep and middle-of-the-night sex, worn with nothing underneath.

She was zipping her jeans when he got back to the living room, and he handed her the shirt. "Smallest one I have."

"Thanks," she said, putting her arms through the sleeves and buttoning it. Suddenly, she looked up. "Shit! Becca's home!"

"So you said."

"I was going to stay with Leigh for those couple of weeks until I close on the new house. But you know her place—she only has that one extra room. If Becca's home, there isn't space."

He held back his smile. Bad news aside, she looked adorable with her hands on her hips and that puzzled frown. "When are we talking about, exactly?"

"I have to be out of the old house in two weeks."

"Stay here."

She looked at him like marbles were falling out of his

ears, banging against the floor. "I'll be traveling," he said, "out west. I actually leave two weeks from today, and I won't be back until after you close on your new place."

"Stay here? For *two weeks*? We can't keep our clothes on while we have dinner for two *hours*."

He crossed his arms and feet and leaned his shoulder against the wall. "Okay, I'm going to call your attention to two things. One: *My* clothes remained on, if you recall, and" —he nodded his chin toward her—"Two: You seem to have enjoyed the removal of yours. But it's irrelevant because I. Won't. Be. Here. I won't even be in the same state."

He could no longer mask his smile. She looked flustered; the offer had thrown her. Deliberate, methodical, in-control Quinn.

It took a lot of willpower, but he resisted the urge to step toward her. By not budging, he hoped to reinforce the idea that they could co-exist in close proximity and not touch.

"Think about it. The offer stands. I won't be home to help you move, so having you use my place while I'm gone is the least I can do. For a friend."

2

ULTERIOR MOTIVES

The truck idled in the driveway's bend as a mover slammed the rear doors. Quinn looked up at the house one last time—the faded cedar shingles, the wavy eyebrows in the roof that covered the front porch, the view. The mesmerizing view—how many hours had the two of them spent over the years watching the ocean? Her heart ached as she said goodbye, not to the house but to the life she and Harris had lived inside it.

She walked around the side by the garage, where she had left the two large peony bushes she dug up earlier, their root bundles wrapped in burlap. One at a time, she brought them to the car, opened the backdoor, and jiggled each until it sat just right in the footwell. She stood and slid her hand into her front jeans pocket, checking. Of course it was still there—she had tucked it deep so it couldn't fall out, the rolled tissue with the necklace from Harris.

That was it. Her roller bag with a few changes of clothes while she stayed at Jonathan's was already in the trunk, along with her laptop, some books, two cartons of photos, important documents, a shovel, potting soil, her old galvanized watering can with the wide sprinkling spout.

The movers would take the rest—furniture, plastic boxes of winter sweaters, linens, dishes, pots and pans, a few keepsakes. She had whittled their possessions markedly the last two weeks; so much had lost its relevance.

She got into the car, keeping the windows down to commit the sounds to memory: tires on the pea gravel, birds warbling in the garden, the faint sound of the surf she could still hear as she turned onto the road.

Three hours later she reached the farmhouse, its dirt driveway the only break in the low fieldstone wall that ran the length of the property. When she had asked the owner if she could plant the peony bushes, he had kindly agreed— although she had yet to formally get the keys.

He would be in the city part of the day, taking care of his grandson. "Come on up," he had said, "make your peonies at home."

She got out of the car, closed the door, and headed down the tree-lined driveway to where it split. To the left, an old brick path veered off to the small farmhouse; to the right, a similar path led to the barn. Brown cedar shake shingles and white trim on both buildings reminded her of the old house, although these had not faded from the wind off the ocean or aged from the salt in the air.

A meadow fanned out between the two paths, sloping gently down to a deck above the river. Boulders dotted the knoll, its grass low, recently clipped. A firepit, its center gray with ash, sat in a clearing of dark silvery stones, a dozen log stumps around it. At the corner of the property lay a stand of white paper-bark birch.

She circled the house looking for a spot to plant the peonies, but no place struck her as the right one so she continued around the barn. The uneven path of bricks wound all the way around it. She stopped at a patch of dirt on one side. In the distance, rolling green foothills framed the view of the river. She shielded her eyes and looked toward the sky. Here the bushes would get good sun. She would be able to see them from the house and from the deck when she sat there to listen to the sounds of the river.

She hurried back to the car, carefully lifted each bush out one at a time, and carried them to the barn. She brought the potting soil next and then the shovel and checked her pocket once more for the necklace.

Sweat beaded on her forehead and back as she dug the two holes. Southern exposure. The plants would definitely get good sun.

When she finished digging, she unwrapped the root ball of the first bush and leveled it in the hole before filling in the surrounding void with loose earth and fertile potting soil.

Before doing the same with the second bush, she knelt and took the rolled tissue from her pocket, carefully unwrapping the necklace. The broken chain dangled from her palm as she brought the pendant to her lips, kissed it, and with tears welling, placed it in the hole.

She wiped the tears and the sweat with her forearm and finished setting the bush, filling the space, pressing the root ball, patting the earth. When she was done, she stood and stepped back to look at them.

The remaining blossoms lolled in the breeze, faded pink. A curious bumblebee flew by, circled, landed on a withered bloom, the petals sagging under its weight. The immediate buzz of life made it seem like the flowers had been growing here all summer long. The bee brushed against lingering grains of pollen, a happy find, the most natural thing in the world.

Against the barn's brown siding, the pink flowers would look beautiful next spring when the blooms popped, full and open in their new home. In a couple of weeks, this place would be home for her, too.

"Look like they've been growin' there forever," a familiar voice said behind her. She turned toward it to see Jerome, the owner, ambling in her direction.

"This was nice of you," she said, shading her eyes again. "Thanks for letting me plant them."

A lick of silver hair fell onto his face. He brushed it back and, with his index finger and thumb on the round tortoise-shell frame of his glasses, lifted them higher on his nose. The tan line on his left ring finger suggested he usually wore a wedding band.

"They must be special to you." He smiled kindly, know-ingly, not waiting for her to answer. "Can I get you something to drink—iced tea, lemonade, wine?"

"Lemonade would be wonderful—it's hotter than I real-ized." She wiped her forehead again.

"Lemonade it is." His eyes fell to her empty watering can. "Spigot's around the corner. Help yourself. I'll be right back."

She watered the bushes, rinsed her hands, and took a seat at the picnic table on the deck. In a couple of minutes, Jerome returned carrying a small tray with two tall yellow glasses. His walk was sprightly, but his eyes sad.

He set the tray on the table, sat across from her, and handed her a glass. "To putting down new roots," he toasted and raised his glass.

"To new roots," she repeated before taking a sip. "Mm,

that's good." An ice cube cracked as she put the glass down on the wood.

"But I must confess, my motive wasn't entirely altruistic."

"No?" She smiled—he was cute, a silver fox.

"I have a favor to ask."

"Aha," she teased. "Ulterior motives."

"But none *too* nefarious."

She liked his vocabulary. "Don't feel obligated," he added. "It's going to be your home soon, but I thought I would check."

"Of course. What is it?"

"I have a vintage car stored in the barn, and I haven't figured out what I'll do with it yet. My new condo doesn't have a garage, and the storage I've looked into so far is"—he whistled and pointed his thumb toward the sky—"exorbitant."

"I can imagine."

"Could I possibly keep it in a corner of the barn for a couple of months until I find a solution? I'm not ready to part with it."

"Sure you can."

He held up his hand, signaling her to wait. "Sleep on it. But if you agree, we would settle on a fair amount of rent."

"It's fine. Honestly, I wasn't planning to use the barn—other than storing gardening tools, I can't imagine what I'd do in there. So your car is more than welcome to stay, for as long as you need."

"I knew I liked you when you first came to look at the place," he said.

They moved on to talk about the property and the town and, when both their glasses were empty, he offered to show her the barn.

"Please," she said. She had peeked in the window with the real estate agent, but it had been hard to see much. Besides, it hadn't mattered—it was the house that had sold her.

They walked around the corner to the tall, wide wooden doors. They slid easily from the shove he gave each one with his body, hardly the heavy, squeaky struggle she would have expected. She stepped in and, as her eyes adjusted to the light, she could see why.

Sunlight filtered through high sparkling windows; a loft ran the perimeter just below them. Although the floor planks were wide and worn, they appeared freshly swept. What had she expected exactly? Rusty door rails? Dust and hay bales? Dry, cracked wood? Cobwebs, bugs, and splinters?

Well, yes, yes, yes, and yes.

But the house had been immaculate each time she toured it, so why should the barn be any different? On one end, Jerome had a lawn tractor, a trailer, and some shovels hanging from a neat row of nails in the wall. On the other end, two white-walled tires peeked out below the bottom edge of a canvas tarp. Behind it was a workshop area, a door with a sign that read—facetiously or not, it was hard to tell—"office," and several shelves of tools, small paint cans, and boxes of auto parts.

She pointed at the tarp. "This must be the car."

"It is. My pride and joy. 1957 Bel Air. Nearly restored." He lifted a corner of the canvas by the headlight. "Do you know antique cars?"

"Afraid not." He rolled the tarp back until it rested on the trunk like a convertible top, open for a summer drive. "But I can see it's something special." Gleaming chrome, creamy aqua body paint, white canvas roof, tail fins. "It's gorgeous."

"Thank you. I started working on her five years ago. It was my future-retirement project. When my wife got sick, I tried to hurry so we could take it out for drives. We went on our first date in a car a lot like this one, many years ago." He brought his hand to the side of his mouth like he was telling a secret. "We kissed in the backseat at a drive-in movie. Cliché, but true."

She didn't need to ask if he finished the restoration in time. It was clear by how the smile lines in his face sagged, by the distance his eyes traveled back in the past, he hadn't.

"I'm sorry," she caught herself saying, although he hadn't actually told her what happened.

He nodded. "Three years ago, almost to the day you first came to see the house. I had a feeling you would be the new owner and that helped me realize that maybe, like my kids and friends have been telling me, it might be time to—forgive the wretched phrase—*move on.*"

"I don't think you ever move on."

"No, I suppose not. I won't pry, but I'm sorry for *your* loss." Harris's death must have showed on her face just like Jerome losing his wife showed on his.

"Thank you. My husband."

He nodded empathically.

"Since it happened, I've been wishing we had more time, but I can't imagine I'd have been ready to say goodbye in another ten years or twenty or—"

"There's never enough time when you're in love." He shook his head.

"No, there isn't," she agreed, watching him absentmindedly run his hands along the edge of the hood. "Will you finish it?"

"I don't know. I should—it's a shame to have her hiding away in here. But it makes me blue to think about what to do when she's done. Taking her for that first ride alone?" Tears pooled at the bottom of his eyes. "I keep wondering what the point would be."

She nodded in understanding and kept her gaze on the car to give him a moment.

There was something about that luscious aqua color.

Aqua.

One of Becca's wedding colors.

Becca's. Wedding.

Barn.

She looked down the length of the wall and, instead of picturing the non-existent bugs and dusty straw, she imagined twinkle lights and large round tables with centerpieces full of flowers, gauzy fabric draped from the rafters, Becca twirling in her gown, looking skyward, while a photographer snapped images from the loft. She pictured friends and relatives eating and drinking, laughing and dancing. She pictured Leigh, who had tried in her own way to support Quinn these past fifteen months, teary with joy at the sight of her daughter—her only child—starting a new chapter of her life.

"I'm sorry," Jerome said. "I didn't bring you in here to be morose." He patted the top of the car. "I wanted to show her to you, since she'll be with you for a while, it seems."

He was quite charming. The thick tortoise frames gave him a quirky, professorial look.

"I understand, trust me. No apologies. May I ask *you* something?" This time, she was the one who didn't wait for an answer before leaping into the story of the wedding venue fiasco and the flash of inspiration she just had about the barn.

As she spoke, she pictured Becca and Charles making their entrance in the vintage car, a *Just Married* sign hanging in the rear window, tin cans clanking as they drove through the massive barn doors.

"I know this is a lot to ask, but do you think you could get the car working well enough so they could use it? Just for a few minutes." She turned and gestured toward the front of the property. "Just to drive down the driveway from the gate. I know she's very special to you, so I understand if you'd rather not. And I may be getting *waaay* ahead of myself, but I think it's the perfect solution for them—the barn, the car, everything."

He clapped and rubbed his hands together, as if ready to get to work. "I'd be honored to finish her in time for a wedding. Reenie would be tickled."

"Fantastic! I'm going to call the mother of the bride."

"I'll leave you to it. I need to run into town to take care of a couple of errands and then I have an early dinner date with some friends, so I'll bid you adieu. Stay as long as you like."

She thanked him and said goodbye, dialed Leigh, and held her breath.

"I have a solution," she blurted when Leigh answered. "For the wedding. Can you meet me at the farmhouse?"

"You're kidding. *How?* Wait, it won't involve a tent, will it?"

"No tents. Bring Becca if she's free. You both need to see it."

"She mentioned she had a meeting this afternoon, but I'll ask if she can get away," Leigh said. "See you in a couple of hours."

"WE HAVE BEEN on the edge of our seats . . . *What* do you have in store?" Leigh asked as she climbed out of the driver's side of her car and shut the door.

Becca did the same on the passenger side, tugging the hem of her sundress down her long, tan thighs. "We have a bet going." Her light brown ponytail, with its loose wave at the tip, swished when she reached to hug Quinn.

"So I want you both to keep an open mind." She motioned for Becca and Leigh to follow her. "It might not feel like the style you were planning at first, but it *can be*. It'll be completely unique. We can get things *exactly* how you want them."

She led them past the freshly planted peony bushes to the enormous barn doorway, stopped, and gestured toward the building with both hands—*here it is*.

Quinn had shown Leigh the house as soon as she decided to buy it, but it had been raining hard that day. They hadn't walked around the property, and Quinn had no reason then to point out the barn. Even if Leigh had noticed it, she would have made some snarky comment about country living and assumed the same thing Quinn had—that it was full of rusty old tools, dust and cobwebs and bugs.

"Voilà. Your very own wedding barn." She pushed hard against the heavy doors like Jerome had, and they slid open. "Go in, have a look."

Becca's expression was curious; Leigh's skeptical, just as expected. "Picture it filled with flowers and tiny lights, organza draped from the beams, tables with linen cloths, nice chairs with fabric drapes, a band or DJ over there"—she pointed—"and the harpist your mom said you hired for the dinner hour right there."

She rattled off each element of the vision that had come

together while she sat on the deck waiting for them to drive up from the city. "How many people were you planning to seat at each table?"

"Ten," Becca said.

"I'm sure we can fit twenty-eight in here, with room to spare for a buffet and a couple of bars."

"And the dance floor," Becca added. A hint of a smile broke out as she went further inside and tilted her head back to look up at the loft.

"You'd get really unusual photographs from up there," Quinn said. Becca nodded slowly and left Quinn and Leigh to walk around.

"Bathrooms?" she called over her shoulder.

"We would have to rent some. I was at a party in the Hamptons a couple of summers ago and the hosts had a chichi trailer with full-size stalls, marble countertops and sinks, the works. I'll make a few calls and find out where they came from."

Quinn led Leigh toward the car at the opposite end. As Becca finished her solo circuit and met them there, Quinn folded back the tarp. Becca's eyes popped wide, and her hedged smile broke out fully.

"The owner said you and Charles can use it to make your entrance," Quinn told her.

"The color, oh my God, it's perfect." Becca's hands came together by her chin.

"Do you really think we can pull off a wedding?" Leigh asked. "It's great, but it's not exactly set up . . . right."

"That's the beauty of it. It's a blank slate. We can make it so chic. And I'd really like to take on the role of wedding planner." Quinn turned to Becca. "It will be my gift to you and Charles."

Becca and Leigh glanced at each other like they were thinking the same thing.

Becca spoke first, seriousness in her eyes. "That's so incredibly generous of you, but Charles and I couldn't let you do it, not after what happened. Wouldn't it be too hard for you?"

"I gave this a lot of consideration while you were on your way here. Nothing will bring him back." She tried to keep her voice from cracking at the simple, tragic truth. "But I wouldn't offer if I didn't want to—with all my heart."

"I wish he could be here, I wish he could marry us," Becca said on a sigh.

Quinn took hold of her hands. "I know, sweetie, I do too."

Harris loved officiating weddings, and he was bananas about Becca. Quinn recalled how he used to help her practice for Mock Trial when she was in high school like it was last week. "He absolutely would have loved the idea of helping with your wedding. Besides, I could use a happy project right now. It will be good for me."

Could use a project was an understatement. She wasn't able to write, she hadn't been back to Octavia's, and she wasn't going to let herself mentally replay sex scenes with Jonathan. Which left, oh, about seventeen waking hours of each day to fill.

Leave it to Leigh to bring any conversation back to business, although she did put her arm around Becca affectionately. "The planner from The St. Martine was going to do *everything*. We'd be starting from scratch," she said to Quinn.

"We have six weeks. I'll make *sure* it comes together." She turned toward Becca. "You can bring Charles up anytime so he can see it before you decide."

"That's okay. I'm in charge of planning. He calls me the wedding domme. And I say"—she looked at Leigh with eyes full of excitement and relief—"this is it. Seriously, I don't know how to thank you, Quinn. Especially after I stole your room at mom's. Sorry about that, by the way."

"Don't give it a second thought."

"It was for the best," Leigh chided, nudging Quinn's arm. "How's it working out at Jonathan's?"

Teasingly, Quinn elbowed her back as the three of them left the barn to head across the meadow. "I haven't actually stayed at the apartment yet—I'm going there now."

Other than a few texts and quick phone calls about logistics, she and Jonathan had talked little since their platonic dinner with benefits. "But he's on his way to the airport as we speak, flying out for a couple of weeks. Sorry to disappoint you."

The sun blazed hot as the three of them approached their cars. Leigh hugged Quinn, then stepped back while Becca threw her arms around her. "Thank you so, so much. Mom always says you're brilliant. *This* is brilliant. Hudson Valley rustic chic. It's going to be the best wedding ever."

3

TIE MY HANDS

The doorman, Barnes, ushered her inside Jonathan's building and handed her the key card to access his floor. "Mr. Jaines said you'll be staying with us for a while. Welcome, and let me know if there's anything you need."

"Thank you," she said as he walked with her to the penthouse elevator, showed her how to use the card, and slid the Art Deco metal grille closed behind her. Despite the antique touch, there was a high-tech whoosh as the car rose, not a rattle to be heard. A few seconds later, it slowed to a halt and the gate slid open.

Her phone rang just as she stepped onto the penthouse landing. She fumbled for it in her bag and answered without looking at the screen.

"Hi, just checking in with you again." It was Octavia, her usually confident voice tentative. The last time they saw each other was at the hospital after Quinn's fall, although she had called a couple of times to see how Quinn was doing. And to recruit her for the club's security committee.

"There's an event I wanted to tell you about. You know

we have that monthly munch—that casual dinner I'd mentioned—tomorrow night."

"Yes, I remember," Quinn said.

"Well, immediately following, we're holding a *101 Intro to Kink* class at the club. We give demonstrations of the equipment on the main floor, and it would be a great way for you to meet more members in a totally no-pressure way."

"Tell me more about the dinner, the munch?" It was on her calendar and she had been planning to go, although as it drew closer, insecurity arose.

"Well, there's amazing food—the member who picks the places is a restaurant critic in her other life—and there's always interesting, animated conversation. Sometimes even about kink."

Quinn liked Octavia's dry humor. "It sounds . . . comfortable."

"It is, and I'll be there to introduce you to anyone you haven't met yet. We can walk to the club together afterward if you decide to join the class."

"I think I'll just start with dinner, but thanks for letting me know about it."

That class sounded intimidating.

They hung up as Quinn passed Jonathan's kitchen, where there was a note laying on the island. If handwriting could be sensual—sexy, even—his was. Clear, rounded, open.

Coffee in pantry, OJ + milk in fridge, clean sheets on bed. Make yourself at home. -J.

Later, after picking up a carry-out salad for dinner and taking a walk around the neighborhood, she wheeled her small suitcase into his room to get ready for bed. It wasn't that late, but today had been a roller coaster of a day.

He had left her a fluffy towel on the bathroom counter.

After a hot shower, she dried off and, in the bedroom, pulled back the duvet to climb into bed. Jonathan's bed. In the oversized shirt he loaned her last time she was here.

She relaxed against his soft sheets. This was nice, the comfort of him without the tension his presence created in her, because it inevitably forced her to think about, to feel, emotions she wasn't ready to invite into her life.

She drifted off, exhausted.

When a wailing siren woke her in what felt like the middle of the night, she glanced at the clock on his night-stand—11:17—and fell back asleep.

In her dreams, the front door opened. Harris was home. She knew this without going to the door. He called to her, searching, wondering why she wasn't in their bedroom in their house by the ocean. She felt his fear at having lost her, heard the panic in his voice. "Quinn? Quinn? You here?"

"I'm here, Har, in here," she called, but her words were fuzzy and slurred from sleep, and he would never hear her, never find her. The door to the bedroom opened, and she startled awake with the sickening sense someone was there.

"Oh, no, I woke you." Jonathan leaned into the room. "And I scared you." Her heart thudded beneath the hand she pressed to her chest. "I kept calling you, so I *wouldn't* do that. Sorry."

"It's okay." She rubbed her eyes and tried to focus. "I went to bed early. What's going on?"

"Flight was delayed. A mechanical problem. They moved us to another gate, twice, and then canceled it. Then we got to stand in line for an hour to rebook. And that was with priority status. But we're rebooked for tomorrow morning. I just wanted you to know I'm here in case you heard me walking around." He gestured toward the living room.

She lifted the sheet and duvet to get up. "Here, you should have your own bed. I'll sleep on the couch."

"Stay. I'm leaving early; I've already woken you up once." He came closer, took the duvet from her and, with his other hand gently on her shoulder, guided her back into bed.

With him standing this close, there were those familiar scents—leather from his bag, mint on his breath—and that voice of his that resounded deep in her body. "Did everything go okay today?"

It felt like days had passed since she left the old house, loaded the peony bushes in the car, and drove into a new life, ready or not. "It did. We resolved Becca's wedding crisis."

"You're kidding? How?" He sat down at the foot of the bed, diagonally across from her. As far away as possible.

She told him how she had planted the flowers, how Jerome showed her the vintage car he was restoring, and how it was this gorgeous aqua color, which was Becca's color, and how it had hit Quinn in that moment that this was the place for the wedding.

"Becca and Leigh drove up this afternoon to see it and . . . problem solved." She snapped her fingers.

"You're unbelievable."

"No, I'm not—it fell into place by itself. I'm sorry you had so much trouble with your flight."

"I'm used to it by now—it's part of the job. Go back to sleep. I'll try to be quiet in the morning." He stretched across the bed and gave her ankle a squeeze through the comforter.

"Goodnight. Have a safe trip."

He shut the door softly on his way out, and she turned on her side and tried to fall asleep.

11:54.

12:39.

She got up and got a drink of water from the bathroom.

1:01.

1:47.

She got up to pee.

2:21.

She laid on her other side, her back, her stomach. But rather than help her fall asleep, each position just reminded her of the things he had done to her body.

She slid one hand past the band of her wet panties and stroked once, twice . . . But what if he heard her?

She got up to pee again and tossed the underwear, with its thin cotton strip soaked through, on the pile of dirty clothes she had left on top of his hamper.

Once back in bed—2:45—she turned the clock away so she couldn't see it and clicked the television on, turning the volume way down with the remote.

A few minutes later, he knocked and cracked the door. "You're still awake."

How could he possibly have heard the TV? "I hope I'm not keeping you up."

"You're not keeping me awake." He came toward her. "Try this. It's warm milk with a splash of brandy and dark rum." He handed the mug to her, keeping one palm underneath it until she had a firm grip.

She took a sip. "Ooh, that's good. Here, share it with me." She offered it back to him.

"Nah, my body never really knows what time zone it's in. I try not to drink when I should be asleep."

"Lucky for me," she teased, taking another sip before setting the mug on the bedside table.

"I brought you something else." He placed it in her

hand. Even in the dark, she could tell by the size and weight and raised buttons against her palm it was a vibrator. "I remembered I had it in your toy bag. Never used. Unfortunately."

She pictured the faded leather bag he had brought to her place every time they were together—and the feelings he evoked with the items he pulled from it.

"I thought it might help you get some rest."

"You're a one-man sleep aid," she joked. What was she supposed to say? "Between the milk and this . . ."

"May I?" He nodded toward the toy.

Please, she thought. "We've talked about this," she said.

"We have. But it's not an engagement ring, it's a vibrator. Do you want to watch infomercials the rest of the night?"

"You're impossible." *For me to stop wanting.*

"How about this? You're holding something to help you get some beauty rest. You can DIY, or I can offer no-strings-attached help—whichever you prefer."

She moved over to make room for him, and he clicked off the TV and lay beside her. She adjusted the pillow so he could rest his head. In the darkness, he found the comforter and top sheet and lifted them. His other hand went to her hip and stroked to the top of her thigh.

Much better than DIY.

"This is exactly how I've been picturing you—wearing my shirt and . . ." His husky voice washed over her, and she drew up her legs so his fingers could find the space between them. ". . . no panties. Damn, Quinn."

"I took them off earlier. They were wet."

"How did you get so wet—what were you thinking about?"

You.

He circled her clit slowly, lightly, torturously with the pad of his thumb. She was already so close—who needed the toy?

He groaned, soft and sexy. "I'm glad I gave you something to think about."

Shit, she hadn't meant to answer him out loud. *How did you get so wet?* Wasn't that more of a rhetorical question?

As he slid the vibe into her, a moan escaped her throat. He angled the toy until one of its ridges pressed that spot inside her. Like a moth to flame, how did he know exactly where and how to touch her?

It began to vibrate, a low deep rumble, drawing a louder cry from her, and she covered her face with the other pillow.

He lifted it off.

"Don't worry, no one can hear you. Except me. And I'd like to hear you again." The vibration stopped, and slowly he removed the toy. Her hips rocked forward, trying to hold on to it. "Not so fast." His hand pressed her pelvis.

She sighed, dropping one of her legs down to the bed. How was she supposed to slow down?

"Turn over." He patted the side of her ass as she shifted onto her belly, and he started to rub her back under the shirt. "Relax," he whispered, his hand flat on her skin, stroking long and slow, from hip to shoulder.

His touch had the opposite effect from the one he intended; instead of relaxing, her need only grew.

"Shhh, relax," he murmured again as he brought his hand slowly down one side of her spine and up the other. She tried to quiet her movements by taking several slow, deep breaths.

"That's better," he cooed, his hand now at the top of her

back, kneading the crook between her shoulder and neck, trailing his fingers through her hair.

She wished he weren't so tender. It was much easier when their interaction was grunt-physical, when she could ignore how his touch stirred something inside her besides intense arousal.

The heel of his hand brushed her neck again, sending a sizzle of current along her skin. *Take a deep breath.*

She imagined raw electricity running down her arm, the current dissipating once it reached the tips of her fingers, dampened by the mattress. With another breath, she relaxed her arms and let the weight of her body sink as he continued massaging.

After she had been still for a while, he guided her onto her back once more. "Close your eyes."

The current hummed again, from nothing more than wondering where he might touch her next. "What are you doing?"

"Shhh. You don't follow instructions very well, do you?"

As she shook her head no, he gently pulled one knee aside and tucked it inside his arm, parting her legs. The tip of the vibrator nudged her entrance, and he slid it deep. The same rumbling, pulsing vibration started anew.

Another loud moan, and she pulled the pillow down over her face once more.

"Oh, no, no, no." He let go of her knee and took the pillow out of her hands, tossing it aside. "I want to hear you. I want to see you."

He continued to work the vibe in and out, unhurried, and she heard herself moan louder and longer with each thrust.

Who was she? Who was *he*? This man who knew the innermost folds and passages of her body, this man with the uncanny sense of how to make her writhe in pleasure, who —even when binding or slapping or fucking her two days' sore—noticed her every movement, the cadence of her every breath.

He kept one hand on her hip now, a connection to let her know he was paying attention, that she could let her guard down. That she could give herself over to sensation, let everything else disappear.

She opened her eyes to watch him—his lips, his eyes, his intensity—and fought the urge to touch his hair, to snake her fingers through it, to run her palms over his cheeks and trace the outline of his mouth with her thumb.

No, she would not slide her hands down along the sides of his neck to feel the muscles and the texture of his skin. She would not caress the width of his shoulders, would not pull him up from beside her legs to feel his weight on her, or bring his head closer so she could inhale his scent and draw his mouth to hers.

"Tie my hands," she blurted, bringing her wrists together and shoving them toward him.

Tie me up so I won't touch you.

She raised her wrists above her head. He let go of the toy and paused for a second, kneeling by her side. His eyes traveled along her torso, up to her hands and down, as if pondering what to use. Then he took the bottom of the shirt she was wearing, his shirt, and without unbuttoning it, slowly dragged it underneath her until he could lift it over her head.

Gathering the fabric, he twisted it tight and knotted it around her hands. Just as the toy began to slip, he moved back down between her legs and pressed it deeper.

This time, he held onto it, intensifying its purr. After a

few seconds, he nudged it further, then back, tiny movements that—

"Let me hear you again." His voice was gravelly with desire.

He lengthened the movements, worked the vibe as if it were part of his body, part of *him*. And that thought, the memory of him inside her, set off another involuntary moan.

"And again," he said a moment later, bringing a finger to her sensitive nub, pressing and circling as he worked the vibe with his other hand. He was taking her to the edge— she was precipitously close—then slowing down, pulling her back, waiting just long enough that she didn't explode the second he resumed touching her.

How did he always know right where she was? She could escape a lot of overwhelming feelings with what he did to her body, but she could not escape him.

She cried out louder and louder, with no conscious effort. Her wrists pressed against his knotted shirt as the wave surged and crested, broke, and dragged her under.

———

HIS DICK THROBBED in time with her hips as he stroked the outside of her body with his thumb and the inside with the vibe. Slow and steady until she came, and then he throbbed to the rhythm of her contractions. He would not have been able to pull that lucky vibe out of her if he were Hercules.

Once her breathing evened out, she turned to him and sheepishly thanked him, then closed her eyes. He resisted the urge to caress her arms, still tied above her head. It had made him even hotter when she thrust her hands at him and begged him to tie them, but as he knotted the fabric, he had second thoughts.

Bound, she wouldn't be able to touch him.

If he were honest, he wasn't after a hand job but to feel her hands on him—anywhere. She could have rubbed his chest or stroked his cheek or . . . *Okay, enough fantasizing. Not going to happen.*

When he untied her wrists and whispered goodnight, she murmured sleepily. He smiled at the sound of her breathing slowing, deepening, as he tiptoed out of the room.

Alone on the couch, he squeezed his pumping fist as hard as he could. In his mind, she straddled him, coming like she just had around the pulsing toy, milking him while she screamed his name.

He came into a tissue, and a pang of frustration soon followed. He wanted something from her she wasn't ready to give. And that little naysaying voice piped up from the depths of his brain, reminding him that maybe she never would be.

He should prepare himself for that eventuality.

As he slipped into sleep, he dreamt a scene similar to the one he had just played in his head. Only this time when they were both spent, she collapsed onto his chest and kissed the notch at the base of his neck before she nodded off against him.

The alarm on his phone went off at five o'clock, and he woke fully erect. But his dick quickly fell limp when he read the lineup of waiting text messages.

Dude. Stomach probs. Bad. NOT traveling today.

That one was from Rich, his production manager.

A second and third had come from his grip and gaffer, a fourth from the field producer, and another from Rich:

Everyone who went out last night is blowing chunks. Will need to rebook team. Tomorrow or day after???? TTYL for update.

They had gone out for drinks and something to eat after the shit show at the airport. Normally Jonathan would have joined them, but he didn't want to come home late and wake Quinn, so he begged off. A wise choice, it turned out. Not only did he avoid getting sick, but he and Quinn had fooled around.

And maybe, in the process, she let a small piece of the wall she was hiding behind fall away.

Yeah, right. He was clearly a little delirious from lack of sleep.

He went to the kitchen to start the coffee. While it brewed, he quietly showered and dressed. Seeing her panties on top of his hamper, knowing she took them off because they were wet from thinking about him, made him smile. It was a sight he could get used to, Quinn's lingerie in his bathroom.

Once the coffee was ready, he poured a cup for himself and left an empty mug next to the machine for her. From his bag, he grabbed a pad and pen, slipped his phone into his pocket, and quietly opened the French doors to the terrace. Out here, he could make calls without waking her.

Sunrise tinted the summer haze pink and purple. An early jackhammer pounded at some nearby construction site; a fire truck horn honked; overhead, a traffic copter rotor beat the warm, humid air.

He loved New York, and Quinn was asleep in his bed.

Maybe one of these days his travel schedule would settle down and he could spend more time here.

The way things had been going, it seemed like the network needed him less and less. *Smile for the camera, J.J. Clay's your showrunner; do what he says.* In other words, *We don't want so much creative input.*

But at the moment, he had a puking crew and an episode or three to pull out of his ass, so he dialed the airline's preferred customer service line to get them onto new flights.

He was still listening to annoying hold music when Quinn came out to the terrace carrying the coffee mug he'd left for her. She had changed out of his button-down and replaced it with full-body coverage: high-waisted yoga pants and a tank top covered by a long-sleeved cardigan-type summer sweater she held closed behind crossed arms. The only skin visible was on her face and neck, the back of one hand, and the tops of her feet.

But if she was thinking clothing would dampen their attraction, she was wrong. At least from his perspective. If all she would give him was feet, well—he imagined holding her ankles and rubbing his cock and balls between them— he could definitely make it work.

"Morning." He held up the phone so she could hear the tinny hold music. "Another change of plans."

"What happened?" She looked around the U-shaped sectional and sat at the other end of the couch he was on. The same couch, at least. That was something.

"They're all sick. The crew. They went out last night after we left the airport. Apparently, their food came with a side of *Salmonella.* I'm trying to rebook everything for tomorrow, but who knows if that'll happen."

"Oh, no. That's awful." That was one more thing he

liked about her, her empathy and understanding. He could tell she genuinely felt bad for them, although him being home made her jumpy.

The airline representative came back on the line. "Still checking, Mr. Jaines. I need to place you on hold again." Quinn gave him a sympathetic look.

She turned and stared into the distance, took a sip of coffee, stared some more. Her wheels were spinning.

"So," she began a moment later, "maybe I should stay at a hotel until you get this sorted out."

"A hotel?"

"A hotel. So you can have your place to yourself."

"Am I making you that uncomfortable?"

"You're not making me uncomfortable. It's nothing you're doing, it's me . . ."

He scoffed at the cliché, and she chuckled. "I know, I know. But it's true. It's just easier for me right now if I keep the boundaries clear. You'll be home for a couple of days and . . ." She picked at a jagged spot at the corner of her thumbnail. "For this arrangement to work for me, I can't accept any more late-night favors—as nice as they are."

"I'm sorry last night made this more difficult. I shouldn't have—"

"Don't apologize. I was a willing participant. But everything is changing, and it's all so . . . uncertain."

Oh, no. Her eyes got that sad look that slayed him.

He should just let her be, let her cry if she needed to, not swoop in to console her. But the instinct to soothe won out. He ended the call, slid across the couch, and wrapped his arms around her.

To his surprise, she leaned against him.

"No more favors," he whispered. He squeezed her shoulder, and she nodded, her hair brushing his upper arm.

"So what's on your agenda today?" he asked after a while, firmly back in just-friends headspace.

"I'm meeting Becca and Leigh for happy hour drinks and appetizers for a strategic huddle with spreadsheets."

"Sounds serious. You seem excited about the wedding. That's something certain and happy to look forward to, right?"

She nodded, enthusiastically. It was nice to see her hopeful about a relationship, even if it wasn't theirs.

"Want to meet back here after you're done and have a light dinner together? There's a great hole-in-the-wall Italian place around the corner." He knew damn well what she would think if he didn't clarify. "Not a date-dinner, just a dinner-dinner. A friends-dinner."

"What, no favors?" She raised an eyebrow, good-natured teasing.

"No favors. You would have to beg, *a lot*, for me to even consider a favor."

She laughed, those big brown eyes sparkling. Damn, that feeling in his chest . . . he was in trouble.

"Dinner sounds good. Oh, wait, I can't. I have that . . . thing I mentioned a while back. Some people from Octavia's are going out to eat."

His neck tightened. She had mentioned it; he had chosen not to think about it.

But it was foolish of him to hope she might be done with Octavia's. He leaned forward, his forearms perched on his knees, thumbs rubbing his forehead, which had suddenly tensed.

"What?"

"Nothing."

"You're upset because I brought up the club?"

He shook his head without looking at her.

"It's a dinner. At a restaurant."

"But it's an Octavia's thing." He kept massaging his eyebrows.

"And that's a problem because . . .?"

"It's not a problem, and it's not my place to say anything. It's just"—aw, hell—"I don't get it. You don't want any 'favors'"—he stopped massaging one eyebrow long enough to make quote marks with his raised index and middle fingers—"but you'll go to a club."

"I'm going out to dinner at a restaurant."

"Yeah, tonight. But . . ."

"I'm meeting up with Octavia and a few other members to have dinner. It's no different from meeting up with my old writers' group or you going out for drinks with your crew. There might even be children sitting nearby." She made a mocking expression of horror, widening her eyes, covering her open mouth with her hand.

"Don't make fun. I don't understand it—we can't have sex, we can't have any messy feelings, but you go to a club? I know what we talked about, but forgive me for not being able to keep up."

"I. Am. Going. To. A. Restaurant. I am not going to the club. Nor am I having sex—not with you, not with anyone else." Her voice softened then. "You've been the only one."

This didn't really make him feel any better. "I guess I just don't get the appeal."

"I want to learn about it. About how it can be so . . ."

"Hot? Sexy? Erotic? Can get you off? Sounds a lot like sex to me."

She sighed, exasperated. "With *you*, yes—it was erotic and got me off, as you so eloquently put it. At the club, it felt good, and I don't mean sexually, to have something else to focus on, to escape for a little while, okay? You're angry now, so you won't understand."

"I'm not angry. I'm . . ." *Hurt. Jealous. Eager to do those things to you myself.*

But he kept his mouth shut. She also was upset, and she wasn't understanding where *he* was coming from.

"This is why there are events like tonight's, why there's a community of like-minded people who get together socially, because other people don't get it." She grimaced and gestured with her hands, like she was straining to pry something stubborn open.

"Oh, so now I'm close-minded, on top of forgetting—as you keep reminding me—that there's nothing happening between us."

She tsked and tilted her head, as if she were about to explain "just friends" and "not ready" to a four-year-old for the umpteenth time.

He preempted. "Look, I have to get back to playing travel agent. I need to get my team's heads out of the toilet and onto a plane or the network's going to air the fucking yule log during my slot."

"Right. I know you have more important things to do than see past your fragile ego and try to understand."

"Oh, I understand, Quinn." He gathered his stuff and stood. "I hear you loud and clear."

4

BIBIMBAP, NOT THE BONDAGE WHEEL

The restaurant's hostess led her on a serpentine path to a table for four in the alcove beside the crowded bar. Quinn put her laptop down and texted Leigh to let her and Becca know where she was.

Leigh replied almost immediately.

Walking over now. There in 5.

The server returned a few moments later, and Quinn ordered an iced tea and an assortment of appetizers to start them off.

When Leigh and Becca arrived, she stood to hug them hello. "Where's Charles?" she asked Becca. "Is he coming separately?"

"He got pulled into a late meeting, so he won't make it. He sends his apologies and said he has complete trust in our decisions."

"He sounds great. I can't wait to meet him."

"He is," Becca agreed, a smile—no, a glow—illuminating her face. She looked like a bride-to-be should look: radiant, elated, optimistic about the future. That's how Quinn had felt before marrying Harris, but she quickly pushed those memories away.

There was no room today for anything but joy; planning this wedding was her gift to Becca, and to Leigh, and she was going to make it flawless.

Quinn angled her laptop so they could see the screen and the spreadsheet she had prepared. After her argument with Jonathan this morning, she had showered fast, gotten dressed, and gathered everything she might possibly need for the entire day. While he made more calls, she slipped out the door and went to a coffee shop to start planning.

She used to use spreadsheets like this one to structure her novels. Only now, instead of beats and chapters and scenes, she filled in the color-coded cells with wedding plot points: cocktail hour, bride and groom arrival, toasts and dinner, first and special dances, cutting the cake.

She tweaked her "Places and Settings" worksheet, too, updating column headings. Seating, buffet and gift tables, bars, flowers, favors, photography, videography, car, music, decorations, lighting. Last but not least, upscale toilet trailers (!!!).

Leigh had been right when she said at the barn that they were basically starting from scratch. It was a lot to pull together but totally do-able.

Two hours later, they had identified and prioritized preferred vendors, each of them tapping away on their phones to look up contact information and flesh out the spreadsheet.

They had talked about the colors and materials and textures, lights and sound, atmosphere and timing. Now they had a plan laid out before them, a plan with brightly colored cells—easy to read, organized, under control.

Quinn glanced at the time at the upper corner of the computer screen, and a kaleidoscope of butterflies took flight in her stomach.

"I have to get going soon," she said, "but I think we're in decent shape. I'll make the calls we talked about first thing tomorrow."

Becca looked at Leigh and then at Quinn, her eyes brimming with tears. "I am so relieved, I can't tell you. I had no clue what we were going to do, and now I feel like it will be even more special, more . . . *us*."

Leigh pulled Becca close and kissed the top of her daughter's head. "It's going to be lovely." She looked at Quinn and mouthed, *Thank you.*

Chairs scudded over the floor as they got up and said goodbye.

"So where are you rushing off to?" Leigh asked Quinn as they left the restaurant. "I thought Jonathan was away."

"He is. Or rather, he was supposed to be, but he was delayed. I'm not meeting him, though. I'm meeting up with a couple of friends for a bite—no one you know," she added quickly, suddenly feeling the urge to check on something, anything, below eye level.

She pictured Leigh's raised eyebrow and disapproving look when their conversation grazed the subject of Octavia's a few weeks ago, and the heated discussion with Jonathan this morning still simmered in her gut. It was just a dinner, that was all. A dinner she neither needed to explain nor justify to people who didn't understand.

───

WITH HIS CREW'S new flights finally booked, Jonathan opened Rich's email with the shooting schedule. It wasn't only the plane tickets that required rebooking; he also told Rich he would take care of rescheduling everything else. Because already they were two days late out of the chute.

Clay, the showrunner, would grouse about the extra money—change and cancellation fees, new permits, surcharges on equipment rentals—the Benjamins would add up.

The show always came in on budget—Jonathan made sure of it, although technically he had been relieved of that responsibility—but the crew was sick, and Clay would have to deal. No one in network leadership was hurting for groceries.

It had been a while since he used the production software—Rich typically sent him a link to the final schedule and call sheets. It sucked to be so hands-off from the day-to-day details, but as Clay had told him many times in varying degrees of bluntness: You're the talent, stay in your lane, the show has people to handle the nitty-gritty, don't worry about that stuff anymore, focus on the script.

Shut up and read your lines.

He scanned the day-one call sheet, then day two, three, and four. This was weird. The places they talked about in preproduction meetings weren't there. Maybe logistically it made more sense to shoot them later in the trip. He clicked through the pages. Day five, day six.

Nada. Not there.

He started a text to Rich, looking up at the entries on the sheets between taps on his phone screen.

What's up with the schedule? The places we all nailed down in pre-pro aren't listed.

What the hell?

And there are others I don't recognize.

Rich sometimes helped out on another Explore show when its staff was shorthanded. Maybe he mistakenly swapped scenes, although that would be really unlike him.

Three dots appeared almost immediately.

No mix-up. Clay asked me to add them. Said we had new advertisers and prospects to feature. I got the impression you were on board. No?

Wonder why you got that impression.

This is the first I'm hearing about it.

Sorry, man. I should have run them by you.

Jonathan's jouncing knee smacked the edge of the coffee table.

Not your fault—it's his call to make.

I'm feeling better—I'll take over and get the schedule back on track. Sorry again.

That's okay, I got it. Rest and hydrate so we can get out of here tomorrow.

That Clay had gone to Rich with changes and not to Jonathan was a dick move.

The saying his mom would share when he was a kid played in his mind: When people show you who they are, believe them. Dick moves mean dick, although Nora would not have put it quite in those terms.

The muscles in his jaw tightened, like they did whenever Clay or Mike, the network's head of programming, pulled one of their stunts. This seemed to occur with more and more frequency, and it was really beginning to irk him.

But he wasn't as upset with them as he was starting to become with himself. The changes they had steadily made with his show were turning it into something entirely different. He knew the stats they recited as well as they did—a lot of viewers liked the show they were creating.

But many old fans, and Jonathan himself, didn't. If he let himself dream for a minute, if he pretended he possessed larger nuts and less fear of screwing up, he would make some changes.

Instead, he went back to the software and his phone to reschedule Clay's new pay-to-play locations.

PREET STOOD by the door of the popular Korean barbecue place near the club. With her head down, a fallen lock of black hair shielded the side of her face while her thumbs tapped away on her phone.

She looked up at Quinn. "Hey, I was just texting you. Octavia asked me to meet you. There's been a change in plans."

"Oh?" Maybe the dinner that had made her jittery all afternoon was canceled.

"Yeah, so, the munch fell apart."

Yesss.

"It's Thursday night in the city and everyone wants to beat traffic heading out east tomorrow, and most of the others who had signed up bailed today because it's so hot," Preet explained. "Octavia's at the club with Alex getting ready for the 101. They're way shorthanded, and she was wondering if we could help. What do you think?"

She looked expectantly at Quinn. "They ordered take-out, by the way, so there will be food. Are you up for it?"

"With setup, sure, I can help."

"Great. Setup and volunteering," Preet clarified.

The butterflies revved their wings in alarm. "Volunteering for . . .?"

"Giving a demo. You know, people go around to each piece of equipment or station and a volunteer explains it. Like, the students take turns leaning over the spanking bench and get flogged and paddled to learn what it's like—it's not play time, just a short demonstration. We rarely get a ton of guests, but of course tonight when the volunteers bail, we have a full house signed up."

"But I have no idea what I'm doing—I should be *taking* the class, not giving demos."

"We'll show you what to do. It's an awesome opportunity to learn. Everyone's there because they're curious, like you. It'll be a good time, I promise. Think of it as public service."

The alternative was going back to Jonathan's apartment early and either continuing their uncomfortable discussion about the club or, not unlikely given his effect on her, fooling around. In either case, helping with the 101 class was the safer option.

Then later, when she got to the penthouse, he might be asleep on the couch since he had an early flight tomorrow. She could slip in the door and tiptoe down the hall, quiet as a mouse.

She hated how he could thrill her one minute—the

neighbors probably heard her scream last night—and exasperate her the next. Why couldn't he understand? She had been clear all along about not being ready for anything serious, anything romantic.

And so what if she wanted to explore, on her own, the newfound appreciation of kink she was discovering? Even if it meant volunteering for an event where she would have to pretend she knew what she was doing when she had no clue.

Her insides rose and swooped with anticipation and fear, like it was the first day of school. "Okay, I'm in."

"Awesome." As they walked toward the club, Preet turned toward her. "So, what's your scene name?" She spoke louder to overcome the clatter and vibration as a subway train barreled below them, underneath the street. "You know, a fake name. For when I introduce you."

"Hmm. I hadn't thought about one."

"How about . . . Kayla?"

"Kayla? Do I look 22?" Unfortunately, though, she did not have a ready alternative.

"It popped into my head. One of my college housemates was Kayla."

"College. See my point? I probably went to college before you were born." It was only a slight exaggeration— Preet looked like she was in her early- to mid-thirties if Quinn had to guess. "But, sure. Kayla works."

"Cool. And, so I know who to introduce you to—if you don't mind my asking—what are you into? I know you're new to the scene but, I mean, dom, sub, both, undecided, TBD?"

"Undecided, TBD." She would have answered differently if Jonathan were involved, but he wasn't.

"It's good to be open. It took me, like, ten years to figure out what I was into."

"If *you* don't mind the question, what *are* you into?" It felt impolite to ask, although Preet had just posed the same question and it hadn't seemed intrusive. Quinn also knew from talking to Octavia and other members that open communication was central to the lifestyle; people spoke candidly about what they wanted—and didn't want—to give and receive.

"I'm a switch. I try to avoid labels, but they come in handy sometimes—as kind of a shorthand."

"So, both roles?"

"Yeah. Mostly top, occasionally bottom."

"Do you have a partner?"

"My wife. It'll be six years next week."

"Congratulations." Preet's expression reminded Quinn of Becca—in love. "She's not into the club scene, that's why you haven't met her at Octavia's."

"She's okay with you at the club, playing with others?" Quinn asked, thinking of how upset Jonathan had gotten when he found her at the club weeks ago, and how the idea of tonight's dinner had riled him this morning.

Not that they were a committed couple like Preet and her wife.

"Pretty much. Sometimes she plays with other people, but privately, not at a club. We talk about it, and we have our lines not to cross, and we each abide by those. It would not have worked in my last relationship, but it does now. And, Ms. Kayla, if I may share Too Much Information, it's hot."

In Quinn's past life, it might have been a tad too much information, but now she welcomed it. "That's actually really helpful to hear. Why doesn't she like the club scene?"

"She's shy, and she's just more private than me."

"Why do *you* like the club scene?" Quinn—Kayla —asked.

"I was interested in BDSM before I found a partner, and the club gave me a way to figure out what I liked. It's harder to do that when you're not in some kind of relationship, you know?"

"Yeah, I get that." Despite her best efforts, she thought of Jonathan as Preet talked about relationships.

"Exploration takes a lot of trust, and if you don't have that kind of safe space in your life with a partner, you can find it at the club. Although I can only speak for Octavia's. It's the only one I've been to. It felt like home the day I walked in the door, so I keep coming back—to play and to help run the front of the house. She's amazing, by the way. Taught me a ton."

"She does seem amazing." Calm, poised, warm, and dialed in to others—but also reserved and private. It made sense. As a pro domme, as the owner of a successful business, Octavia had a role to play—at the club, she would *have* to put her real self away.

"So, what's your deal, Ms. Kayla? Are you in a relationship?"

"No."

Preet's head swiveled toward her in an instant. "That came out fast."

Quinn laughed. "It did, didn't it? It's complicated. And whatever it is, the club apparently is a sticking point. I've tried to explain that it's not about sex for me. It's been more about how my brain shuts off for a while."

"Otherwise known as subspace." Fitting timing. They reached the brownstone and one at a time opened the app on their phones to register their arrival and unlock the door.

Preet gestured for her to enter first. "That's why a lot of us are here."

TONIGHT, Octavia's didn't look like Octavia's. The bright overhead lights were on, the dreamy music was off, some of the dungeon monitors were moving furniture and dragging chairs to the edge of the room. Others prepared individual stations—a spanking bench, a cage, a St. Andrew's cross attached to a large wheel.

The backstage feel and hum of activity gave the club a theatric, pre-curtain vibe.

Alex stood near the center of the main floor talking to Octavia and scrolling on his tablet screen. When he spotted Preet and Quinn, he motioned them over. "Can you cover the cage?" he asked Preet. "And, Quinn, can you take the bondage wheel?"

"Kayla!" Preet interjected. "Her scene name's Kayla."

"Got it. Kayla, you're at the bondage wheel." He tapped his screen once, dramatically. *There, done.*

Octavia watched her, perhaps guessing Quinn hadn't come up with the name herself. But it didn't matter—it was only a nickname, and it could be changed. Just like her outfit. The people scurrying around her wore latex and leather, complicated-looking strappy things, tall black boots. Quinn's slacks and silk blouse, appropriate for a casual weeknight dinner out, did not fit in tonight.

"Kayla was expecting bibimbap, not the bondage wheel." Sheepishly, she gestured at her outfit. "Do you have more appropriate clothes I could borrow?" Maybe the club had a lost-and-found box of kink wear stashed under the front desk.

Octavia's smile was enthusiastic. "Do I have clothes?" She motioned toward the stairs. "Follow me."

Her private office took up the entire top floor of the brownstone. A bathroom occupied one corner, a hotel-like kitchenette in another. A domed skylight graced the center of a round ceiling medallion, giving the space the sense of even more height. Her furniture was elegant but minimal—a large antique desk, a modern sectional couch, a rose velvet chaise longue.

On one side, long wine-colored curtains just like the ones at the club entrance hung from a rod along the soffit.

Octavia parted the panels so the two of them could pass through. A horseshoe of clothing racks, coat trees, and shoe shelves lined the recessed space. Another chaise held clothes draped over the back, with a pair of shoes on the floor nearby. One lay on its side, giving the impression it had come off a tired foot.

Octavia's closet.

"Help yourself to whatever you feel comfortable in." Her gaze traveled down and back up Quinn's body. "I think most of what I have should fit you, but there's fabric tape and safety pins in the desk drawer if you like something that needs a quick alteration." When she opened the top center drawer, Quinn also spied a roll of thin leather cord, black ribbon, scissors, string, and adhesive bandages. "What shoe size do you wear?"

"Eight."

"Kismet." Octavia pointed to a tall rack that held, by rapid calculation, a hundred pairs. A wooden step stool allowed access to the higher shelves, a library of footwear.

"I have to get back downstairs, but take your time. I so appreciate you agreeing to help tonight. You'll be great."

"So, um, what exactly do I need to do?"

"Change, and meet me on the main floor. I'll show you. Easy-peasy."

Octavia parted the curtains again and breezed through while Quinn browsed, bypassing the lingerie and costumes for a rack of fetish wear. She settled on a stretchy black dress that offered the most coverage and fewest tricky straps and, from the shoe shelf, platform sandals with a chunky heel.

The memory of her high heel catching in the grate her first night here shimmied in her mind, and she pushed it away before it materialized.

After a final check in the gilt-framed floor mirror, she whisked her hands past her shoulders to loosen the hair stuck to her sweaty neck, then put on some lipstick and hurried downstairs.

Octavia was about to lead a huddle in the middle of the main floor. "Okay, everyone. Ten minutes 'til show time. We'll stick to the usual schedule." She glanced at Quinn. "So for those of you who are new, I'll give a brief talk about the club's history and the importance of safe words—we'll use the red, yellow, green system tonight—and consent and communication. I'll open it up for questions, and then our guests are free to roam the floor."

With a few clicks of her remote control, she turned off the bright overhead lights. Soft illumination emanated from beneath the crown molding, giving the space a subdued, fleecy effect. Ambient music began to flow from hidden speakers. The volunteers jogged to their stations, some taking last-minute swigs from their water bottles as they got into position.

Quinn went to the bondage wheel, a black metal spiderweb with a padded backrest and restraints for hands and feet. She unfastened the torso straps as Octavia glided over for her quick lesson.

It was pretty straightforward, she had to admit, at least for tonight's purposes. Ask if the "bottom" would like to wear a blindfold. Help them step up onto the wooden platform so Quinn could reach the cuffs on the spokes. Bind their hands, buckle each foot. Don't spin the wheel, just joggle it to the left and to the right, enough to convey a sense of what it would feel like in motion.

From the black tote bag Octavia had brought over, she pulled out several blindfolds, a long downy feather, a leather slapper, and a small serrated wheel with a handle—a Wartenberg wheel, Quinn had learned courtesy of her internet searches the last few weeks.

"Once they're bound, and blindfolded if they want to be, you can demo these but only on exposed skin on their arms and legs." Octavia showed Quinn how all three felt, although the slapper she already knew well from Jonathan.

Not going to think about that.

Octavia moved skillfully, confidently, and Quinn had a million questions that had nothing to do with tonight's demo. But now was not a good time to ask her; participants with eager, inquisitive expressions started to fill the seats. "We'll talk later. Kayla," she added with a wink. "Break a leg."

THE BONDAGE WHEEL must have intimidated people. A snaking line had formed for the spanking bench and the kneeler and to learn from Octavia how to wield a whip. "Nurse" Alex stood beside an exam table in a white coat, with a half-dozen men queued up to experience stirrups.

The wax demo, rope station, a paddling from the "principal" over a retro metal desk—they, too, had drawn considerable crowds.

If the club used signs like theme parks to let visitors know the wait time at each attraction, Quinn's bondage wheel could offer an immediate ride.

Maybe her nerves were giving off a newbie vibe. Stepping away from the wheel, she widened her stance and put her hands on her hips, power posing as she scanned the room for a volunteer to entice.

Her strategy wasn't working. No one seemed to notice her or her eight-foot-diameter wheel.

Except for the man in the full black face mask coming toward her in a tight black shirt and even tighter black pants, an outfit that left little about the girth of his biceps—or other parts of his anatomy—to the imagination.

His eyes were a focused, determined brown, she could just about make out through the small eyeholes as he came closer. Together with his look, his carriage, they screamed dominant. An experienced one.

Just great.

He extended his hand. "Maximillian, longtime Octavia's member, longtime dom." He spoke with a British accent, his voice coming through a narrow slit by his mouth. "And you are?"

"Kayla." Suddenly she was relieved to have the scene name. It had seemed so unnecessary only a half-hour ago.

"Pleased to make your acquaintance. May I?" He gestured toward the wheel. She might be fresh on the scene, but she knew he meant her; he wanted her to bottom, to be put on the wheel. "Perhaps if the others see you, they'll be more likely to come over and watch. Otherwise, they might worry you'd pick them to volunteer."

Valid point, although still she hesitated—she was supposed to be leading the demo. But he had experience she lacked, and she did not want to let Octavia down with the dearth of activity at her station.

"Sure, why not?"

His mask bulged below his prominent cheek bones—a smile. "Splendid. What's your safe word? Something easy you'll remember if it gets too intense."

His question caught her off guard. Playing with Jonathan had happened so organically, they hadn't realized they should have a safe word. Not to mention he read her so well, he would have just known if something were wrong or she needed to stop. *Don't go there.*

"Red."

"Red, it is."

With a job to do, she stepped onto the platform, and Maximillian buckled her wrists and ankles. It felt awkward, raised above the ground, spread-eagled.

She glanced at the small round table that held the items Octavia had left, and she tensed when he picked up the blindfold. "Can I interest you in wearing this? It will give spectators a more realistic portrayal. And heighten the experience for you—a veritable win-win."

Anything to help draw some participants and help her feel less self-conscious about that newbie aura that surely surrounded her. "Okay, yes."

He put the blindfold on, careful not to tangle her hair. "Let's get started then, shall we?"

She nodded. "Let's." In no time, they would have a crowd, she was sure of it.

He rotated the wheel a quarter turn to the right, more than Octavia had told her to turn it, until it felt as if she were lying on her side. He rotated it further and slightly faster the next time, and it felt like a swan-dive through the air.

With each full revolution her body rose and fell, a figurehead on a ship's bow as it arced through the waves, slow to rise, fast to fall, slow to rise again.

Weighted, weightless.

The pattern relaxed the tense muscles of her face; the pull of gravity on the downward turns dulled her nervousness.

Her position in space was clear for five or six—or was it more?—revolutions, and then it grew harder to tell where she was.

Had anyone come over to watch?

As if she had spoken the question aloud, he answered while he continued to rotate the wheel. "It seems we're still alone, Kayla. Would you like to go on?"

Maybe people would finish their stints at the other stations and begin to wander over. "Yes."

"Ah, good girl."

His words clawed, fingernails on a blackboard. "Don't call me that." The tickle in her throat from speaking while upside down made her cough, and he quickly righted her, then brought a bottle of water to her lips so she could take a drink.

Calling her a good girl was inappropriate. She might not have much experience in the club scene, and he might be a dominant, but he wasn't *her* dominant.

"My apologies. Watching your subtle reactions has been quite entrancing, and I slipped. Thank you for reminding me of the boundaries. I hope I haven't ruined our scene. Shall we continue, or would you like to stop?"

It struck her that his accent sounded artificially stiff and was probably fake, the accent of someone who wanted to project power and control and thought a fake British accent was the way to do it.

He reminded her of a character. In one of her early books, she had written a villain, a sympathetic one, who had had a tortured past and now possessed a hyper-ambitious drive. Not a drive for money or fame, but for power. To wield enough power to ensure he and his children could create a different future, a new legacy.

She couldn't remember the character's name at the moment; her mind was fuzzy, in a not-unpleasant way. The name wasn't important anyway, but Maximillian had made her think of him.

"It's okay," she said. "We can continue."

"Splendid."

Now the wheel was turning again, and soon something brushed the outer edge of her foot, which jerked against the restraint when she automatically tried to move it away.

The feather.

He tickled and traced her foot, brushed along her arches, her calves, around her knees and up the front of her thighs, scattering waves of awareness throughout her body. Her scalp tingled as her hair brushed the floor.

His breathing grew deliberate and heavy. If she were writing their scene, this moment would be the midpoint, where the tension rose, where the situation turned serious.

The tickle was replaced with the sting of pins and needles as he dragged the spiked instrument along the sensitive skin on the underside of her arms. The touch of the cold, sharp metal sent a shiver through her, and her hand jerked against the wrist cuff.

He turned the large wheel again, and her hair now hung sideways, like the weight of her cheeks and of her breasts inside Octavia's stretchy top, pulled by the force of gravity toward the center of the earth.

Suddenly, she heard a loud clap against her outer thigh —*son of a bitch*—before a sharp bolt of heat radiated from the point of impact.

The slapper.

He was watching her, she could feel it.

Thwack.

He did it again and again, the heat spreading in expanding ripples, sensation in three dimensions.

Her hair shushed over the platform as he turned her again and continued to strike: Her arms, her legs, and, a few times, her hips.

If she let her thoughts go a little more, she could sink into this, let it spread over her like a blanket of quicksilver, let it press her into nothingness.

The movement of air whispered through the fine hairs on her arm. He was going to slap her again.

If Octavia's voice beside them didn't stop his motion.

"Maximillian, let's wind down. This isn't playtime."

"As you wish," he said curtly, slowly rotating the wheel to bring Quinn fully upright. Only then did she hear Octavia's boots click-clack away.

Without speaking, he undid the blindfold and the buckles and helped her down, keeping a hand near her elbow. She concentrated on anchoring the soles of her shoes to the floor; her legs felt less than steady.

"What do you say we continue on our own sometime, Kayla? I usually play upstairs, on level three."

The mask that obscured nearly all of his face. The rapid effect of what he had just demonstrated on her. The mention of the explicit area of the club. Her insides turned queasy. "I'm not here for that kind of play," she told him.

He leaned closer, tilted his ear toward her, like he didn't believe he heard her right. "You're not here for what?"

"Anything upstairs or, you know . . . sex. I'm not here for sex."

His dark eyes rose skeptically toward the edges of the mask's holes.

She gestured around the room, where plenty of couples and small groups milled about, while her brain went to Jonathan. Blindfolding her, binding her wrists, touching her, teasing her, and . . . *Stop*. "The club isn't about that for me."

"Then what *is* it about?"

"Sensation . . . Mainly, the escape."

"Sensation, subspace—at least I presume that's what you mean by 'escape'—and no sex. Hmm." He rubbed his chin pensively. "That sounds like a challenge I can accept."

"I'm not issuing a challenge." She made sure to look at him directly when she said it.

"I understand. But consider it, Kayla. Let's learn to trust each other more. Down here in the PG-rated playground if you like—I'll make an exception."

AS THE 101 wound down later, Quinn found Octavia in her suite on the top floor. She was sitting on the edge of the chaise, looking at her phone. "I'm sorry about that," Quinn said, standing near the velvet curtain. "My job was to show off the wheel, and I ended up needing a rescue."

Octavia patted the cushion beside her, an invitation. "Don't apologize—members can be a bit . . . eager . . . when there's someone new. You know I can't say anything about particular individuals, but a word to the wise: Some members might be better to play with once one has more experience."

Quinn undid the ankle straps of the heels she had borrowed. "Got it. Thanks for the heads up. Hey, can I ask you something?"

"Sure can. Anything."

Quinn aligned the shoes on the floor beside the chaise, then sat up to face her. "He wanted to play upstairs, on level three, and I said I wasn't here for sex." Octavia gave a listening nod, her expression somewhere between neutral and sympathetic, not unlike the therapist Quinn had seen shortly after Harris died. "Is that so unusual?"

Octavia's dark corkscrew curls swung like a skirt ruffle when she shook her head. "Not unusual. BDSM can be highly erotic, but it doesn't have to involve sex. Whether it does depends on what you're doing and why and with whom you're doing it. We have quite a few members in committed relationships who come to the club without their partners. Some have open relationships, and some come here to play without sex. I can't tell you names, but as you get to know people, you'll learn their stories."

"I talked to Preet on the walk over tonight, and she shared some of her situation. It helps to hear."

Octavia sat a smidge taller, like she had an idea. "Come with me—I want to show you something."

Quinn followed her through the velvet curtains and down the hallway to where it overlooked the floors below. "How many people do you see on the main level?" She gestured downward. "A rough estimate."

Quinn quickly surveyed. "I don't know—fifty, eighty?"

"Right, and it's a weeknight, so it's quieter. At the very least, that's the number of reasons there are for learning about and practicing the lifestyle. Many of those reasons involve sex, and many don't. Other than abiding by some of the key principles you already know—safety, consent, communication—there's no *right* approach. Think of it like fast food. You don't have to buy the whole combo meal, you can simply order the fries."

Quinn laughed. "Great analogy. Jonathan keeps saying he doesn't get it. I'll have to borrow your line."

"It's all yours. He doesn't get the lifestyle, or your interest in it, or you joining the club?"

Octavia was perceptive. "The club. Our play was sort of an accidental discovery—for both of us. But I guess it's irrelevant now. We're . . . just friends."

Which meant he had no right to be possessive or jealous. Jealous was reserved for lovers, partners, girlfriends, wives. Besides, she wasn't doing anything sexual with others at the club. Was it so different from getting a massage or taking a private yoga class?

Octavia's face wore that therapist look again, and it was easy to keep talking. "I'm not ready for another serious relationship, and it's not fair to be intimate and expect no one to develop feelings." She looked down at her hand and pushed back a cuticle. Jonathan wasn't the only one who had developed feelings.

There was something about Octavia's demeanor that helped Quinn cut to the chase, even with things she didn't necessarily want to acknowledge. "At least not more feelings than we already have, that *I* already have."

Octavia nodded sympathetically. "And how do you deal with those feelings?"

Quinn pointed toward the floor below. "I come here."

They both laughed. "A healthy strategy, but I might be biased." Octavia rested her arm on the railing and turned toward her. "At the risk of complicating your life further, here's something to think about. My mentor, Madame Manon, lives outside Paris. Every summer, she hosts a gathering of her protégés. She would welcome a guest, although—I'll be honest—I've never brought anyone. But I trust you to be discreet, and it would be a fantastic learning experience for you. Would you like to come with me?"

Quinn's eyes widened with disbelief. She had read about Madame Manon in that old magazine profile of Octavia. It was hard to remember details now, but there was some fabulous estate with over-the-top parties. The woman had been a dominatrix for, if Quinn recalled, close to a half century. "You're inviting me to come with you to Madame Manon's château in France?"

"Yes. You can get as involved as you like, but if you only want to observe from a quiet corner of the room, you can— no one will pressure you. Madame is a marvel, and one could do a lot worse than spend a few days in Paris with her."

How could she possibly accept? She was so inexperienced, she would be completely out of place. "I couldn't."

Why not?

"Why not?" Octavia asked.

"I'm organizing a huge, last-minute wedding for a family friend, and it will take up nearly every waking moment of the next few weeks."

That sounded so lame. Apparently she had time to be here, and to stew about her issue with Jonathan.

Octavia offered a wan smile. "You want to learn, and the retreat at Madame's is a wonderful educational opportunity. But either way, let's continue the conversation. If I'm not on the floor next time you come in, you can always text me."

"I appreciate the invitation, I really do. If the timing were different . . ."

"No worries—I understand."

Quinn's gaze dropped, and she realized she was still wearing Octavia's dress. "I should change before I leave, but I'll take it with me, have it cleaned, and drop it off in a couple of days."

"Keep it. It suits you." Octavia gave a little shrug. "And, who knows, you might need it again sometime."

5

SLICK WITH SOAP

Planning Becca's wedding reception had blurred the last two weeks, along with most of Quinn's non-wedding-related thoughts. *Bingo.*

She and Becca and Leigh made a formidable type-A team, and Quinn was proud of their not-so-small wins. Like finding the boutique Hudson Valley bakery a few towns over that crafted The. Most. Gorgeous. Cakes.

Simple and elegant, the tiers brushed with just a sheen of frosting so the layers showed through, distressed and white-washed, draped in a spiral of edible flower blossoms, no sweating pastel fondant in sight.

The shop was booked solid for Becca's date, but Quinn cajoled the owner, who generously agreed to stretch capacity and make it happen. She also recommended a florist-friend of hers, whose artistry turned out to be phenomenal. Becca had watched, transfixed, as the woman pulled together a centerpiece arrangement—a gorgeous mix of local and rare flowers with iridescent glass pearls as vase filler that, when the light hit, perfectly matched Jerome's vintage car.

Tonight, the three of them were out having dinner. Charles again had begged off, some last-minute work thing. Their mission was to put finishing touches on the playlist and first dances and to review recommendations from the DJ and sound engineer about the acoustics in the barn.

Anyone watching them huddled over their laptops, occasionally pausing to take a bite of their meals, might have assumed they were leading one of Charles's high-stakes corporate mergers or developing architectural plans for a Manhattan skyscraper.

At least until Becca began doing the hand choreography to "Y.M.C.A.," careful not to knock over her wine, and Leigh hummed a few bars of "Sweet Caroline."

Becca's phone chimed with an alert and she turned it over to look at the screen. Her brow tightened and she sighed. "Poor Charles. His meeting's running long; he won't be home until late."

She typed a reply, added a puckering emoji with a heart, Quinn could see, and set the phone down with another sigh. "We so need this honeymoon. The pressure he's under is not sustainable. I can't wait for us to unplug."

Leigh patted the back of Becca's hand. "It's hard, sweetie, but think of what he's working toward—taking over that family's private equity group? He *is* under a lot of pressure because that's a huge, huge endeavor."

"I know, mom." Becca, one of the least materialistic people Quinn knew, slipped her hand out from under Leigh's. Quinn guessed Becca would much prefer to have Charles more available with less disposable income than to prove to his father and uncle he was worthy of leading one of the city's largest investment firms.

They finished up the playlist and the last bites of their food. When the server brought the check, Leigh put her credit card in the black portfolio pocket and, with what Quinn recognized as deliberate nonchalance, asked, "So, when is Jonathan back?"

"A couple more days, I think. We haven't been in touch much."

Leigh's eyes lasered in on hers. "Why not?"

"Because we're both busy? He's shooting, and I'm closing on the new house tomorrow, moving the day after, and there's this, um, wedding coming up? There's not much reason to be in touch, anyway."

"I beg to differ. He's sexy as all get-out, and he's very interested in you. I'd say those are two compelling reasons to be in touch."

Quinn shoved aside the image of him licking molten chocolate from her belly. "We text now and then, mostly about apartment stuff—you know, mail that came for him and how the thermostat works."

Leigh gave her a pleased look, with one eyebrow cocked. "Very domestic."

When the three of them said goodbye outside the restaurant, Leigh and Becca turned right, while Quinn went left, toward Jonathan's place.

The bitter taste left by her last discussion with him was fading, in part because she kept telling herself it didn't matter whether he understood why she went to Octavia's. And in part because every few days he sent her a quick text or a photo from the trip. The connection, from his safe distance miles and miles away, was nice. And didn't push their contentious buttons.

Their. As in shared buttons.

Like she had told Octavia after the 101 class, they were not a couple. They were friends. She wasn't ready for more right now. If she ever would be, who knew?

It occurred to her that the pattern of these thoughts was not so different from how she would write the internal monologue of a character who was trying hard to convince herself why the safe choice was the way to go, why she really didn't want or need the more risky thing—all while assuring herself the rationale was airtight.

Completely airtight.

One more city block until the empty, air-conditioned apartment, a glass of chilled wine on the rooftop terrace, and solitude. They would all help quell the thoughts.

Barnes greeted her and opened the door, a bead of sweat oozing down his forehead. It might be nine or ten o'clock at night, but the humidity still hung heavy. She could not wait to get out of these sticky clothes.

Inside the cool apartment, she slipped off her shoes, shrugged off the light blazer that had protected her from the restaurant's air-conditioned chill, and set her bag and phone on the kitchen island. White type flashed on the black screen. Preet.

At O's. Are you coming in tonight? BTW, Maximillian is here. Asked about you. Trudged upstairs looking disappointed. If you come, O and I will protect you.

Not tonight. Hate to disappoint him.

If there were a fake-sad emoji to match Preet's tongue-in-cheek tone, she would have used it. Scening with Maximillian again seemed . . . dangerous.

Not that they had actually scened; it was a demonstration. But Octavia had issued a subtle warning, and Quinn would take it to heart. Besides, the rapid effect on her of how he commanded the wheel was unsettling—as was the mask and his invitation to level three.

She set the phone down again and peeled off her damp t-shirt, bra, and jeans as she made her way down the hall. In the bathroom, she hung the clothes on the towel rack, put on a camisole top, and headed back to the kitchen. From the refrigerator, she took the bottle of Chardonnay and poured what remained into a wineglass.

As she dropped the empty bottle into the recycling bin, the bag of pretzels on the counter caught her eye. She stole the big yellow clip that held it closed, gathered and twisted her hair upward, and clipped it in place. Resourceful perhaps, but it was good, very good, that no one was around to see her.

On the terrace, she settled cross-legged on the sectional and took a sip of the chilled wine. Her thoughts roamed— the house closing tomorrow, moving plans, the wedding, the flash of disappointment on Becca's face when she read Charles's text about tonight being another late night, Leigh's comment about Jonathan's interest.

And then the thoughts yielded to memory: the electric current of his touch, how even blindfolded she could sense his gaze on her, feel his weight on her body, hear his voice, his . . . *voice.*

Deep and resonant. "Quinn. It's me."

Her hand flew to the base of her throat as she turned. He was standing by the French doors in the dim light, and her eyes took him in as if they had a mind of their own, from his long legs and narrow hips up to the widening triangle of his broad chest. "What are you doing here?"

"I was able to change . . . We wrapped early. I texted and called so I wouldn't barge in on you again."

He was coming toward her.

"My phone's inside, sorry. You're not barging, you live here." Now he was standing behind her, and he pressed a hand on her shoulder, bare except for the strap of her cami. His touch was light, but intentional.

"You doing alright?" he asked, not moving his hand away.

The clip in her hair threatened to come loose when she nodded, so she reached back and readjusted it, careful not to brush the front of his jeans with her fumbling hands.

God, she must be a sight, sweaty and half-naked. The terrace was partially covered, shielding her from the view of apartments in other buildings and, assuming she would be alone, she hadn't bothered to put on shorts.

She felt his eyes on her, listening for her answer. "Yeah, things are . . . things are coming together."

She used to write books with dozens of chapters, tens of thousands of words, but now she was having trouble putting a handful of them into one coherent sentence that actually conveyed substantive information.

"Great. Becca excited?"

"Thrilled." She turned and looked up at him, her words slowly returning. "We hit the jackpot with unique artisans for the cake and the flowers, and her music will be great and . . ." she paused, trying not to notice his hand against her bare skin.

For goodness' sake, he was touching her shoulder. It did not get more platonic than a shoulder. "You'll see. You're coming right?" She hadn't seen Becca's full guest list, but of course he would be there. "You can bring someone. You know, a plus one."

Why on earth had she just said that?

"Good to know." She could hear the corner of his mouth quirk from his tone. He let go of her shoulder as he came around the couch, moved her glass of wine to the side of the coffee table, and sat down to face her. With his forearms on his thighs and hands folded by his knees, he was barely a breath away. "Wild horses couldn't keep me from Becca's wedding. But I'm attending without a guest."

Sweet relief.

But if he were involved with someone, good for him. She wanted him to be happy.

-ish.

"The woman I'd like to bring is busy that night," he said.

Something in her gut dropped. She nodded rapidly. "Mm. Mm hm." She didn't want to hear more, so she squeezed her mouth, which seemed to have had a strong sense of its own agency a second ago, shut.

"She's running the show, but I hope she'll have a few minutes to spend with me—or to dance—at some point that evening."

She let out the breath she hadn't realized she was holding, and a smile broke free. "Okay, yes. I'm sure she'll make time for you."

"Good. Because before I left, I was kind of an oaf. I've been hoping she'll forgive me."

His thumbs were antsy, and she laid her palms over his clasped hands to quiet them. "She forgives you." Whatever anger remained from their talk two weeks ago dissipated, shimmery heat waves off hot asphalt, into the charged space between them. What replaced it was the funny feeling that filled her chest as she looked at the man sitting before her— his relieved smile, his kind eyes with their corner laugh lines, his full, soft lips . . .

"Are we okay?" he asked.

"We're okay."

"Good. Listen, I'll try to keep my feelings under wraps.

Your friendship is important to me, and I don't want to jeopardize the relationship"—he put his hand out, urging her not to react—"lower case r, that we have."

"I don't expect you to get it. I don't fully get it myself, but there's no reason for you to be jealous." She put her hands over his again. "It was completely different when it was with you, but I can't . . . be with you . . . right now. It's too soon." *Too soon to move forward and too late to go back.* "Like I've said."

They had been to this place before, reaching some level of understanding about the club or, at least, agreeing they didn't fully understand the other's perspective but accepting it, and then—*poof*—another argument.

"Sh, sh. I know. I know," he repeated, more softly. "Let's not rehash." Her hands were resting on her thighs now, braced. He picked them up and laced his fingers through hers, bringing their arms up between them. "No arguing?"

"No arguing. It's too hot, anyway."

"Hey, since I'm home, I can help you move. I figured you could use an extra set of hands."

Hands. These hands, the ones holding hers. She could imagine them on other parts of her body, caressing up and down her back, or drawing her arms up over her head while he moved inside her.

"I could—" she cleared her throat and swallowed hard, "definitely use . . . hands. To move." She unlaced her fingers from his and dropped her forehead into her palm, her cheeks growing even hotter by the second. "Sorry, I think the heat is melting my brain."

His laugh reverberated through her body, jostling something way deep in her chest.

HE HUSTLED to the bakery around the corner, the first customer at the door when they opened at seven a.m. Two buttery croissants, two whole-grain blueberry muffins—he was curious to learn which she would prefer, although he would not find out today.

When he got back home, he brewed coffee and put the baked goods on a plate. The shower was running, and he fought like a gladiator to keep the mental images at bay. Quinn in his bathroom, naked and wet, her body slick with soap.

Down, boy.

He poured most of the coffee into a thermal pitcher, the rest into a travel mug, tore a paper towel to wrap a croissant, and put it in the outside pocket of his work bag. On a sticky note he pulled from the stack in the kitchen drawer, he wrote "Good luck today!!!" and pressed it to the counter next to the coffee jug.

He wasn't sticking around to share breakfast. He needed to focus on preparing the talks he would give in Paris—sustainable tourism, how to travel more authentically, meeting locals—topics popular with audiences at industry events like this one, but getting harder and harder to cover in any kind of genuine way, especially given Clay's influence on his show.

That's why he was going to sit on a park bench or in a coffee shop or, last resort, his office, even though his network digs felt less comfortable by the week. Being in the same space as Quinn was distracting. So was thinking about her, but at least removing himself from her presence would lessen the effect.

Last night at the Vegas airport, the gate agent had called him to the podium to tell him his standby request for an earlier flight back to JFK had cleared. Once he stowed his bag onboard and took his seat, he called Quinn and, when she didn't answer, texted her so he wouldn't surprise her again. Then he leaned against the headrest and tried, unsuccessfully, to get comfortable. The agent had offered him an upgrade if a seat opened up in first class, and he declined out of habit. He never took upgrades when he traveled with his crew. Dick move to sip champagne in the front cabin while the rest of the staff, who busted their asses, were forced to imitate contortionists in coach.

He had re-arranged the schedule with Rich to finish his scenes early. For the rest, including the ample supply of B-roll backup footage Rich smartly insisted on, the crew would work without him anyway. He wanted to get back to New York to help Quinn move, although he had not and would not tell her that.

When he got to the apartment last night, it was clear she hadn't heard his voice mail or seen his text, or she would not have been sitting on the roof deck, sexily sweaty and mascara-smudged, in panties and a spaghetti-strap top. Or using his snack bag clip to keep her hair off her neck, her long, sexy neck that would be damp and taste of salt, with a few loose, dark strands framing her pretty face.

He had wanted to touch her, stroke her cheek and— maybe someday, in some alternate universe she would invite him into—bend closer and kiss lips that welcomed him, lips that said, *I missed you, I'm happy you're home.*

He had not failed to notice the way she looked him up and down as he stood by the terrace doors or how she got tongue-tied. Her reaction seemed to be about more than surprise at his early arrival, at least that's what he wanted to believe. If he had made an overture, if he had wound his fingers through her hair and tugged teasingly, if he had nipped at her shoulder, or brought her hands behind her like he did when he bound them, she might have jumped right in.

But then afterward, she would back away and, guaranteed, she would not let him help her move. The move was a big step for her, and more than sex, he wanted to be included in this next part of her life, present at its inception.

But he would not tell her that either. He would not risk scaring her away. No, he was just a friend offering another friend a coupla extra hands.

Besides, there was only so much rejection a man could take.

He was done putting himself out there; she would have to make the next move. No longer would he initiate only to get that metaphorical slap in the face when she ran off to the club and reminded him they were Just. Friends.

He found a bench in a shady, less-traveled corner of the park. Sunglasses on, he worked on the slide decks, inserting photos and video clips and practicing each of the presentations from start to finish—in his head, so no one called the cops at the odd guy talking and gesturing to himself.

The area grew busier, prompting him to glance at the clock on his screen. Lunchtime. He took off and grabbed a sandwich to take to the office, where he ran through his talks again all afternoon—with Rich, a couple of other crew members, and finally, one of Explore's communications managers.

This last trial run was to make sure he didn't say anything they didn't want him to. What that might be, he didn't know exactly, but lately marketing had to sign off on all his material—unless someone other than him had written it.

The office had cleared out by early evening, and he hung out at his desk a little longer, reviewing and scheduling approved social media posts, editing video, going through the presentations yet another time.

By nine, his brain fried from so much screen work, he closed the laptop, slid it into his bag, picked up a takeout dinner, and took it up to the High Line. He loved it up here —the views, the people-watching, the artwork, the glimpses of everyday life through the building windows. Had Quinn been up here? Even if she had, he wanted to show her something she hadn't seen—a garden, a sculpture, a new vantage point.

All day, he had done a great job busying himself with work, but now, up here, he missed her.

Her closing on the farmhouse was today. He had stopped himself from texting to ask her how it went; he needed to give her space. If circumstances were different, he would have chilled a bottle of champagne and suggested they go out for a nice dinner, a subdued but deliberate marking of the event, but not a celebration.

If Harris were still alive, Jonathan would not be part of her life. She never would have sent his car away that first night; she never would have turned to him. He should not forget; he was the lucky beneficiary of a dead man's grieving wife.

Her choosing him was a lot like being cast for the show and his marriage to Delphine, once-in-a-lifetime opportunities that fell into his lap unbidden, unwarranted. Opportunities one didn't question aloud or ask much of lest the giver of the good fortune realize their mistake and swipe it all away.

Quinn would go to bed early tonight. Her practical, organized self would want to get a full night's sleep before the move tomorrow. But he also knew she would feel blue. He wanted to shoulder some of the pain, lie beside her in his bed and spoon his body around hers, sweep the hair off her face, kiss her temple before they fell asleep.

That was the fairytale version.

Instead, he waited until after eleven to go home to the silent apartment, careful in the dark bathroom not to drop anything that would make noise while he got ready to crash on the couch.

6

SALT AND CARAMEL

The stone farmhouse with the royal blue front door was just as Quinn had described, an offbeat blend of old and new. The wide-plank pine floors dated back a couple of hundred years and creaked in spots he quickly learned as the two of them ferried boxes all day. Dark, rough-hewn beams stretched across the white ceilings, and wooden doors with gnome-sized knobs still held antique keys in the keyholes. In the kitchen, a nice gas range filled the stone hearth. It was easy to see why the place had charmed her—it was having the same effect on him.

He brought the box he was carrying to the second-floor room she chose as her office. When he came down the stairs, she was plugging in a lamp in the foyer. She lifted a brown carton from one of two piles, put it back, then lifted the top box from the other stack. Checking the weight, if he had to guess, because she opted for the lighter one. Balancing it on her knee, she tilted it to read the label on the side.

"Here," he offered, jogging down the last few steps, "Let me."

"Oh, I didn't see you there. It's dishes, so that way." She pointed toward the kitchen. "Thanks."

She followed him through the living room, past another fireplace, and into the kitchen, where he set the box on the marble-topped island in the center of the room. The box cutter was in the pocket of his jeans, but when he went for it she told him to leave it.

"It's getting late," she added, sounding tired. Her disheveled hair that was usually smooth as silk, the frayed knees of her old jeans, the V-neck t-shirt that hung off one shoulder—she looked tired, too. "Let's order some dinner."

She slid a takeout menu out from behind a magnetic disc on the enormous fridge. "And I should check the train schedule," he said, reaching for the phone in his back pocket. As if on cue, a train whistle blared from somewhere along the tracks that paralleled the Hudson River. "But I'll come back first thing in the morning to help you finish."

"You don't have to take the train home tonight—there's an air mattress in one of these boxes . . . Somewhere." Her index finger found the curve under her bottom lip and her brow furrowed. Adorable. She looked around the room, then at him. "Did you see the packing list?"

He bit back a smile.

"What?"

"Nothing. It's just . . ." He should probably keep quiet.

"*What?*" she asked again, smoothing her hair and moving it over her shoulder self-consciously.

He feigned a serious look, although his grin must be betraying it. "Did you just invite me to spend the night?"

She laughed, and his chest grew warm. "I guess I did. Technically."

"Okay. Just checking. Technically." He leaned against the counter and crossed his arms. It was that or hug her.

She pointed the folded menu toward him. "Air. Mattress."

He gestured nonchalantly with one hand. "Eh. Details." Okay, he was definitely grinning.

She called and placed their order—Chinese food— massaging the side of her neck as she spoke. When she ended the call, she looked around at the boxes and her shoulders rose and fell as she sighed.

"They'll still be there tomorrow, don't worry," he said. "I have an idea." He stepped toward her and turned her around, put his hands on her shoulders and began walking her toward the stairs.

She was probably thinking he wanted to take her to bed. Which was an outstanding idea, but not what he was planning.

"Wha . . ."

"Relax, I'm drawing you a bath." He let go of her shoulders as she walked up the stairs in front of him and placed his hand lightly on her lower back when they reached the top.

"I really should keep unpacking," she said, but her hand went straight to the sore spot she had been rubbing a moment ago.

"Take a break, Quinn. You've been at it for hours." He stifled the urge to massage her neck and, instead, nudged her toward the master bedroom, with its fresh white walls and more dark beams. Clothes on hangers covered the bed, waiting to be hung in the closet.

Her bathroom had a large open shower and a huge oval soaking tub made of cedar, surrounded by a ring of smooth stones. It reminded him of the *ofuro* he bathed in when he had shot several episodes in Japan.

He knelt and turned on the tap, adjusted the temperature, and put the stopper in place before standing back up.

She was leaning on the countertop a couple of feet away, watching him. "Come here," he said, reaching for the hem of her t-shirt.

"I can undress myself, but nice try," she teased, her big brown eyes darkening a hint.

"I know, but you're tired."

She crossed her arms and started to lift the bottom of her shirt overhead. "Ouch." She winced as her hand flew to her shoulder. "Okay, okay. Help me take it off."

She moved toward him, and he lifted the soft cotton and pulled it over her head, careful not to look at the white lace triangles that held her two perfect breasts.

Next, he undid the button of her jeans and brought her hands to his shoulders so she wouldn't lose her balance as he worked them down her legs.

"I can do it." As she said it, she brought one hand from his shoulder to her chest to cover herself.

Crouched in front of her, he looked up to meet her eyes, again trying exceedingly hard but mostly failing, not to look at anything in between. "I've seen you before, remember?"

His mouth, sandpaper-dry, was level with her belly button, and he closed his eyes to better focus on the task at hand. He needed to anti-passionately—was that a word?— remove her pants, not draw his tongue over her stomach to taste her smooth skin, or work his way upward and touch those breasts or downward to inhale her scent and dip . . .

Focus.

Her cheeks reddened right before his eyes. She moved the hand that had been partially covering her chest to his shoulder but avoided looking at him. Sheepishly, she smiled and brushed the sides of his neck with her thumbs. "I remember."

"Good." He liked to razz her once in a while, not to make her uncomfortable but to remind her they had shared something—something important.

When her pants were off, he occupied himself with folding them while she angled her upper body toward the tub and took off the bra and, he noticed out of the corner of his eye, her panties.

With his hand at her elbow, he kept his eyes firmly on her shoulder blades while she climbed the two wooden steps to the tub.

Shoulder blades should be a safe place to rest one's eyes, but this was Quinn, and she was naked.

He bit his lip and took her hand while she stepped in as the tub continued to fill, steam rising around her, which helped to cloud his view. She settled onto one of the benches.

Room enough for two.

She leaned her head back against the tub wall, closed her eyes, and let out a long, deep breath. "You were right. This was a wonderful idea."

"I'll find you a towel."

In the bedroom, he checked the boxes until he found one labeled "Towels and sheets—master" and cut the tape with the box cutter from his pocket. It was no longer the only hard thing in that vicinity, and he willed away his arousal before returning to the bathroom.

He draped the bath towel over the side of the tub, careful to check that it didn't reach the waterline. "Thanks," she said without opening her eyes. The notch above her top lip glistened with droplets condensed from the steam.

"Sure," he croaked. "I'll go wait for the food."

It might still be August, but a late summer chill edged into the evening air, and he sized up the living room fireplace. There was some ash in the firebox—good, it wasn't just decorative—and he looked up the chimney to check that the flue was open. And since the wood in his pocket was not the right sort, he went outside to search for logs and some kindling. A house with three fireplaces must have a woodpile nearby.

He found cut and neatly stacked logs on the side of the barn, gathered some twigs on his way back to the house and, once inside, built a fire.

The doorbell rang just as she was coming down the stairs. Her wet hair looked even darker than usual, and it had dripped onto her baggy t-shirt, leaving a damp patch near each shoulder. The band of her faded pajama bottoms was folded over so they didn't so much rest on her hips as appear to float there in a way that made him think how easily they might come off.

He opened the door. "Mr. Layborn?" The delivery guy held out a large brown bag that smelled a lot like Jonathan imagined heaven might. Too many hours had passed since lunch.

"Yep, that's ours," he said, opting not to correct his name.

"Plates and chopsticks for you and your wife in the bag," the man said, handing it over.

"And this is for you. Have a good evening." Quinn had paid with her credit card when she ordered, and now Jonathan handed over a few bucks' tip.

He didn't look to see Quinn's reaction to the delivery guy's choice of words, although he sensed the man's assumption smarted.

The glass top of the coffee table from her old house leaned against the living room wall, heavily protected by bubble-wrap and duct tape, so they sat on the floor, their backs against the couch. He opened the flaps and placed the white containers between them, then handed her a paper sleeve with chopsticks before tearing open his own.

She doled out the spring rolls and took an eager bite. It was good to see her hungry and eating. From the morsels of time they had spent together, he knew food often was a low priority.

They ate in comfortable, easy silence, punctuated by approving murmurs. When he tasted a dumpling, the bright flavors of ginger and lemongrass burst in his mouth. "Mmm. You have to try this."

Using the chopsticks, he dipped the remaining half in the sauce and brought it toward her with one hand. With the other, he held the container underneath to catch any falling drops.

"Open," he said, guiding it to her mouth. She tried to get closer, putting her hand on his wrist as she moved, but she jostled them both and the dumpling splash-landed, sending salty droplets flying.

"Sorry!" She wiped her cheek and used her napkin to dab a few drops from his.

He put the sauce and chopsticks down. "You missed one."

With his thumb, he rubbed a splatter off her cheekbone. "Two actually." He wiped another near her temple with the pad of his ring finger.

Her eyes were closed and she looked lovely and although he didn't notice any evidence of sauce there, he caressed the apple of her cheek.

She placed her hand over his, holding it to her face. Her eyes opened, her gaze searching, for what he wasn't sure. Although as usual he had his hopes.

He kept his hand still on her cheek, enjoying the warmth of her palm, their relaxed closeness.

After a moment, he brushed her cheekbone with the smallest sweep of his thumb. "You doing okay—with today, I mean, with the new house and everything?"

"Somehow, I am." She nodded and gave him a sad smile that made his chest clench. A second later, the scent of the damn raspberries from her hair wafted its way from his nostrils to his groin. It wasn't that the fragrance reminded him of their amazing sex.

Okay, it wasn't *only* that.

The more powerful effect was in how the intimacy of this moment hit him: of sharing takeout Chinese on the floor, of Quinn just out of the bath, her hair still wet, wearing an old t-shirt, of her holding his hand to her face, of how being so close to her made his pulse gallop.

HE WIPED the sauce off her face. Was she ever a major klutz tonight, and . . . did he just caress her cheek?

His hand was warm and soothing, and she kept it there, relaxing into it. He stroked her cheekbone and asked, low and sweet, if she was doing okay.

"Somehow, I am," she said. "It helps that you're touching me."

He looked surprised. It wasn't the kind of thing she should say to him. She didn't want to encourage anything, but it was true—there was something about him, about how they were so easy together. He didn't make her forget the sadness, but helped her be present in it and see a glimmer beyond it at the same time.

"At your service. Moving sucks." With his free hand, he

moved the cartons of food from between them and carefully scooched closer to her, keeping his palm right where it was underneath hers. He moved slowly, gently, like he was trying not to startle her.

She must seem so skittish and fickle. Come here, go away; I want you, I'm not ready.

She leaned her head against his upper arm and touched the front of his shirt, her fingers tingling at the thought of his bare chest beneath.

"Thank you," she said, pressing her hand against him. "I *am* doing okay, but I probably would have fallen apart if you hadn't been here today."

He put his arm around her shoulder. "I doubt that. Do you feel like falling apart now?"

"At the moment, no." Slowly, she shook her head. "It's just . . . This place is home now—I know that—but it feels surreal."

"Of course it does. It's a tremendous change, all of it. But you're stronger than you give yourself credit for. You would have done fine today. It wouldn't have been easy, but you would have done fine. I know it."

He stroked her cheek again, just one light swipe with the side of his index finger, and wove his fingers through her hair near her temple. It released the heavy scent of her conditioner, and he inhaled sharply.

"It's really strong, sorry."

"Don't be sorry. It's one of those smells that evokes . . . vivid memories." His eyelids looked heavy as he lifted another lock of her hair, let it fall, and inhaled again.

"Of?" She kept her eyes on him. He was thinking of a person, a woman. Maybe it was Delphine, or maybe the girlfriend.

His Adam's apple rose when he swallowed, and her

fingers wandered up to touch it, then to touch the side of his neck. He tilted his head toward her, shaking it slowly from side to side, like she was silly for missing the point. "Guess." The fusion of his deep voice and the sensation as he rustled her hair when he inhaled again made her insides quiver.

Oh.

Her. He was talking about her. So she wasn't the only one whose memory had been etched with their brief history.

And it was getting harder and harder to ignore what the future might hold for them. Their intensity went beyond sex. She leaned closer and rubbed his chest, the shirt fabric warm from his body heat. Her fingers found the embroidered letters of the monogram on the pocket. JPJ. "What's your middle name?" she asked.

Non sequitur much?

"Poul." He spelled it out, P-O-U-L.

"After?"

"My father." There was the tiniest droop at the corners of his eyes. Sadness. She had been so consumed with her own grief and need, she had paid little attention to his feelings, his history, his life.

"You would have liked him," he added, "and he would have *loved* you. He was a big reader—in fact, he read some of your books. I wish you could have known him."

"Me, too," she replied, "although I feel like I kind of do." She rubbed his chest. "When did he die?"

"Eight years ago."

Eight years. Long enough that people would stop expressing sympathy, although Jonathan clearly still felt a deep loss. "I'm sorry. I can tell he was a good man."

"He was." His chin rustled the top of her head again.

His voice was lower when he spoke the next time. "One

morning, he just didn't wake up. Cardiac arrest. It would have been quick, which I'm grateful for, but it was a real shock. And I was in Asia, so it took a long time to get back home. That's the only trip I've ever regretted."

He continued stroking her hair as he spoke. "The weekend before it happened was his brother's birthday and if I'd been home, I would have been at the party and gotten to hang out with him one more time."

"I'm sorry," she repeated. What else was there to say? Tenderness welled inside her at seeing his regret, his pain. It eclipsed her reticence and fear, and she reached for him, put her hand around the back of his head, felt his skin, his hairline, the small patch of stubble where his ear met his jaw. With her head tilted up into the crook of his neck, she inhaled his scent and kissed the skin there. He trembled, and the vibration moved through the two of them as she brought his face closer to hers.

He was right there, his caresses of her hair slower now, the air between them charged and expectant. She traced his lips with her index finger. They were warm and textured and soft. His breath tickled her nose.

The wall that had held back her feelings since that first night gave way, and when she brought her mouth to his, he tasted of salt and caramel.

At last, a kiss.

An overwhelming feeling of relief flooded and immediately surprised her, as if her subconscious had finally gotten what it longed for.

His hand found her elbow and traced down her arm until his fingers entwined with hers.

"What's this?" he whispered, his voice dampened by the corner of her lips, where he was softly kissing, before rubbing the skin alongside her mouth and cheek lightly with his nose.

"I think it was me kissing you." Her voice sounded raspy, and her heartbeat thudded in her ears when she rested against his chest. With the strong pulse she felt through the cloth of his shirt, it was almost too much, this rush of physical sensation and emotion.

He cradled her head against him, his rib cage rising and falling with each shallow breath.

"I've touched and tasted every part of you, but not your lips, your mouth," he said, his thumb outlining the bottom curve of her lower lip, and she dipped her head to kiss it, her fingers finding the fleshy part of his palm.

"Kissing is the most intimate thing." She lifted her gaze to meet his, then leaned against him again and closed her eyes. She pictured them in bed together, how distant she had made herself—her body with him, but her heart, her mind, her soul far away.

"Incredibly intimate," he whispered, nodding. "Thank you." His arms tightened around her.

"I actually fainted the first time Harris and I kissed." He sighed and pecked the top of her head.

Why, exactly, had she shared that, of all things? "I'm sorry, I . . ."

"Shhh, no sorries." He took hold of her hand. "It's fine to talk about him. I want you to. I want to know everything about you, and he is a huge part of you."

Is. He got it. He understood how, even though Harris was gone, he was still very much with her. He made no demand to "move on," no ultimatum to choose between the past and the present.

"Come on," he said, planting a quick kiss on the back of her hand. "Let's put the food away and call it a day."

She was grateful for the knowing way he lightened the moment, and it freed her to verbalize what she suddenly knew she wanted. "Would you do something for me?"

He leaned his torso back and looked at her head on, cupping her face in his big, comforting hands. "Anything. What do you need?"

His intense gaze made her warm, his closeness like light focused through a prism. "Sleep with me tonight? No, I mean . . ."

Playfully, he tapped the tip of her nose with his index finger. "I know what you mean. You can share my air mattress any time."

She laughed and softened into him, and he rocked her ever-so-gently side to side. His lips brushed her head near her ear. "I'll hold you all night."

———

THE TRAIN WHISTLE keened far in the distance; there was still plenty of time for their car to cross the tracks. "I love you, honey," Harris was saying as he turned toward her. Over his shoulder, beside his sweet face, she saw the train bearing down on them. How did it get here so soon?

The whistle howled, louder and louder, until it exploded into spinning darkness and new sounds—glass shattering, metal twisting, bones breaking. Harris fell heavy against her, making it hard to breathe. She tried to rouse him. "Wake up. You're okay. Wake up." His arm dropped beside her, leaden.

She screamed at him now, desperate, furious, panicked, and tried to shake him awake, kicking her feet against him, pushing and tugging him with her arms, frantic for him to move, to show some sign of life.

The weight released, and someone rolled her over and shook her shoulder. "Wake up, Quinn."

Jonathan.

"You were having a nightmare. It's okay. It's okay," he repeated.

But it wasn't okay. Nausea filled her as she sat up and crossed her arms over her stomach. The images, the sounds, they flickered in her mind like an old movie. She fisted her hands and pressed them to her eyes, trying to make it stop. Jonathan was sitting up beside her, rubbing her back.

"Open your eyes, Quinn." He stopped rubbing and reached for something.

"Here, put your socks on. When I was a kid and I had a nightmare, my mom would walk me around. It helps you forget the dream." He got up, came to her side of the bed, and helped her with the socks. "Come on, let's walk."

With his arm around her waist, they went through each of the downstairs rooms, eventually circling back to the living room. He stopped by one of the tall windows, unlatched the sash, and opened it wide to let in the cool air.

The moon was a sliver—a shiny yellow sticker pressed to a wall of darkness. A cricket chirped, and an animal trilled, maybe some type of owl?

They were in that crevasse in the dead of night, after man-made noise quieted, before the birds began their pre-dawn chatter. In a few hours, it would be morning in this new house, in this new life. What would daybreak sound like here?

He guided her by the shoulders to stand in front of him, and he wrapped his arms around her. "Any better?" His whisper rustled her hair.

"A little. You're right—the images are fading. But the feeling . . ." She brought her hand to her stomach. Dread, terror, sorrow. They were all still there, eager students shooting up their hands during roll call, here, here, here.

"I know." He touched his lips to the side of her head, behind her temple. "I know," he repeated, more softly this time. "I wish I could make it better."

"You do." She entwined her arms with his and leaned back against him.

Together, they stared quietly into the darkness. It reminded her of that first night, how they stood side by side, also looking out at the night ahead of them. They were barely touching then, but the air between them held something impossible not to notice.

Impossible not to feel.

"Can I make you some tea?" His lips were by her ear again, sending a warm shiver through her.

Warm shiver, wasn't that an oxymoron? Why did he have to affect her in ways that defied physics?

"That's okay. Let's go back to bed," she replied. He led her back to the air mattress and covered her with the sheet, then went to the fireplace, added a log to the fire, and stoked it.

Once the flames leapt again, he got into bed and faced her. She touched his shoulder, traced through his t-shirt along his collarbone to his chest. Whole, unbroken, strong.

SHE WOKE up with her cheek on the pillow of curls on his chest, soothing and scratchy at the same time. It was the perfect metaphor for him; even groggy, she could see the symbolism, her most tender source of healing also her greatest threat. He felt as right as anything could feel after

Harris's death, this man who brightened her life and also held the power to devastate—what if she lost him, too?

It was not being alone that she feared. She had always loved her solitude. Except for an occasional bout of loneliness, she had been content on her own before she met Harris. No, what she was so afraid of was falling in love with another man and having her life again shattered to bits.

How many times could she let her heart break? There would be no putting the fragments, bent and misshapen, back together a second time.

As she lay against him, three words took shape in her mind that she would need to hold fast to: *Don't love me.*

She rolled off the air mattress quietly and tiptoed to the kitchen to start coffee in the machine they had set up last night. It sputtered and steamed, the scent mingling with the lingering smell of woodsmoke from the fire Jonathan had made to keep them warm. She pulled aside the thin linen curtains that hung over the sink and peered out the window. The view framed the barn and the newly planted peonies and a few fallen leaves that skittered across the grass in the wind.

In the distance, another train whistled, its sound lower and shorter than the one she must have heard in her sleep, the one that set off her nightmare. It would be a passenger train carrying commuters into Manhattan, not a long, loud freight train barreling through her dreams, tearing a new hole in her life.

Jonathan's bare feet padded on the wood floor, slowing as he came to stand beside her by the sink. "Morning," she said, turning toward him, his hair tousled from sleep, his soft t-shirt wrinkled. "I was trying to be quiet so I wouldn't wake you."

"You were quiet, but it was hard not to notice you left

the bounce house." He pointed over his shoulder with his thumb at the air mattress with the rumpled sheets and pillows side by side. "It sounded like you slept. No more nightmares?" His hand found the curve of her neck and he stroked her skin, just once. "It seemed like a terrible one."

That sickening feeling from the dream washed over her again. "That was the only one, but, yeah, it was bad." Bad enough that she hadn't expected to fall back to sleep after, but—ensconced in his arms, her cheek against his body— soon, she did.

She touched his chest just below the ridged collar of his t-shirt. He was looking at her lips, his head bending toward hers so slightly she wondered if it was deliberate. Quickly, she lifted her hand and turned away to get two mugs out of the cardboard box on the counter.

The newspaper wrapping left smudges of ink, and she rinsed the mugs under the tap. He stayed beside her, and her hand suddenly felt less sure around the ceramic cup than it had a second ago. As she poured coffee and handed the mug over to him, she kept her elbow close to her side to keep from shaking.

Why was this so uncomfortable?

As if sensing her unease, he backed up and leaned against the other counter before taking a sip. Finally, he stopped looking at her like some specimen under a micro-scope and glanced at the nearest pile. "What do you say we grab a quick breakfast in town and then unpack more boxes? I have some work things I need to do later today," he went on, "but I can take care of them from here this afternoon."

"That's alright—I'm not hungry and, besides, I need to settle in by myself. I'm going to live here on my own, so . . ."

"Okay, but I leave for Paris in a couple of days. I won't be around to help."

"Really, I'm fine. I'll do a little at a time," she told him.

"I know you can handle it, but I want to help." His forehead was starting to furrow. "How about tomorrow? I can come up after work and give you a hand for a few hours, bring some food for dinner—"

"Jonathan. I said it's okay." Her response came out harsher than she intended, and she tried to soften it. "I won't be home much tomorrow, anyway."

"You are the dream wedding planner—that's impressive dedication. Becca won the jackpot with you."

"What? Oh. Actually, it's not wedding stuff. I'm helping out at Octavia's." She looked at the floor and the stacked boxes and the floor again before glancing at him.

His face told her he wasn't happy. But this was his issue, not hers, and certainly not theirs to share, together.

Not a couple.

"Do you want me not to tell you? Would you rather I lie?"

"No, of course I don't want you to lie. But seriously? With all you have going on right now, you're going to—"

She cut him off and looked directly at him as if daring him to pick another argument over this. "Yes."

"You're starting a new life here." He gestured around them. "Why do you need to be so involved with the club?"

"Because my so-called 'new life'"—she waggled her index and middle fingers, quotation marks around sarcasm —"includes the club. That's why. I thought we put this discussion to bed already. Are we going to have it again?"

"I guess we are because I still don't get it. I mean, I get that you're grieving—and there's no timeline for that. But," —he brought his hand to his forehead, swiped the top of his head, and blew out a breath—"what is that place for you, some kind of alternative grief support group?"

Her pulse pounded even harder in her ears at his low blow. She breathed in to steady herself, but it was shallow; anger tightened around her rib cage.

"Why does the club bother you so much? I told you, it's not about sex for me, there. Just because *you* make everything about that doesn't mean I do."

"Wow. If I recall, it was you who sent Gil away that night with my ride; it was you who wanted to have sex. You wouldn't talk to me, you wouldn't kiss me. You couldn't have made it more clear that all you wanted was to fuck."

"You're right. That's all I wanted that night. To fuck. So sorry I twisted your arm. I didn't realize you really wanted to play house—and therapist. So, Dr. Relationship, about last night? We didn't move in together. We didn't set a wedding date. We kissed. So what?"

She turned away and stared out the window.

"*So what?*" He exhaled loudly behind her, and she pictured how his nostrils would flare, how he was probably shaking his head in frustration and rubbing the back of his neck. "Maybe *you* can't feel anything unless there's hot wax dripping on your body or you're being slapped, but I can," he spat. "I felt how you opened up to me last night. And that night after my flight was canceled, and the night you came over for dinner, and plenty of other nights. You can say whatever you want, but I *felt* how you reacted."

She pressed her lips together so she wouldn't bluster any more. That was a serious pet peeve of hers, when someone lashed out with a nonsensical argument to deflect something they didn't want to face.

It had not been just a kiss. She could still feel how their lips, their mouths, their tongues explored and tasted each other, how their connection had an energy all its own, how it hummed in her body and, she could sense, in his.

But she also still felt other things: guilt at kissing another man for the first time and, even more strongly, the bone-deep fear of losing him too. And those emotions wound tendrils around her heart like a parasitic vine.

She kept her eyes trained out the window, still not turning to face him. He stood stock-still for a moment, giving her a chance to respond, but she kept her mouth shut. It was only when she heard him start to walk away that she looked. He was shaking his head again as he headed for the living room couch, where he had draped his jeans and shirt last night. Quickly, he pulled on the faded denim, zipped the fly, buttoned his shirt.

Fine, just go, she wanted to yell. *Please, don't leave.*

She would not cry. She kept her back to him until she heard the front door open and slam. This sinking, sickening feeling as he left her house was exactly why she couldn't let this go any further.

This was what had to happen. It was the best thing—the safest thing—for both of them. More kissing, more sex, more enjoying each other's company, more soothing bad dreams in the middle of the night—the feelings would only grow, and the risk of potentially losing it all was just too high.

Don't love me.

That's what it came down to.

Because I can't let myself love you back.

She dumped his coffee in the sink and unpacked a box, the first full of plates, the next one pots and pans. She ripped off the tape from around the glass top for the sofa table and tore through the padding, balled it all up, and pelted it across the room. A knotted piece of sticky tape clung to her hands. Fuck!

Fuck. "All you wanted was to fuck."

No, you're wrong, she should have told him: I wanted to disappear.

The whole damn day stretched before her, hundreds of minutes of fighting to keep her mind from going places she didn't want it to go.

She ran upstairs and got her laptop out of the bag in her office and opened the wedding planning spreadsheet. All the intense work so far meant they were in decent shape; the wedding was still a few weeks away. Most of the remaining tasks she could take care of in the next few days: reconfirming the change in venue with the contractors, getting in touch with people who hadn't RSVP'd, signing off on final proofs from the printer for the place cards and signs, putting the gift bags together, a few odds and ends that undoubtedly would crop up. Overall, nothing too time-consuming, nothing prone to complication. Her other major task—unpacking and getting situated here in the house—what was the hurry? She had whatever time remained of the rest of her life.

It wasn't ideal timing but if she didn't do this, she would regret it, and not only because she would be here with the memories of how Jonathan's lips had felt against hers playing on an exasperatingly endless loop. She needed to do this for both of them, to cut him loose and stand back from the slippery edge, safe from the eddy of intensifying feelings. She needed to find her way forward without him.

Phone in hand, she scrolled through the contacts until she found the number, then tapped the call symbol.

Octavia answered, her voice friendly and warm. "Is it too late to accept your invitation to Paris?" Quinn blurted. "I'll have to meet you there and leave a couple of days early, but I would like to join you."

7

SHOW ME

The applause buoyed him, amplifying the adrenaline rush from a live audience, a roomful of *Spice of Life* fans. They may not have been the fans from his early years, but they were fans nonetheless.

He had almost forgotten how effective the exhilaration was at, temporarily at least, clearing his brain of the "You got lucky, don't fuck it up" chorus. For as long as the high lasted, it was just him working the room, sharing stories from around the world, photos, and his observations on traveling. For as long as the high lasted, despite the network's changing target demographics and the helicopter-parenting, it was just him connecting with his audience.

That he knew how to do.

The timing was perfect. He needed this today after how he and Quinn left things right before he had left for Paris. He thought he could keep his feelings about the club under wraps; apparently, he could not. But telling her the truth about why it bothered him so much was impossible—saying it would have been the end of them, of their relationship as it were, right then and there.

Her words had burrowed under his skin like some infectious worm. *Playing house. We didn't set a wedding date. We kissed, so what?*

He thought he understood defense mechanisms, but still, what she had said that morning was brutal.

Add jet-lag-induced insomnia to the whole ugly mix, and he had felt like crap pretty much up until the moment he splashed on some sponsor's shitty cologne and left his hotel room for the convention center.

At least right now, with the presentation remote in his hand and an enthusiastic crowd in front of him and online, the crappy feeling was gone.

Now the moderator, the head of marketing from another sponsor, was collecting questions from the in-person audience and reading others off her tablet from the live-stream chat.

No direct questions from the audience. That was one of Mike's hard and fast rules—questions had to be screened in case they referred to Jonathan's affair, or as Mike cleverly phrased it, "the past."

Questions from Lucinda in Minneapolis. Wei. Ainsley. Ghedi. Esme from here in Paris. The Q&A ran over the allotted half-hour, until the moderator wrapped it up. Jonathan pretended to go off script—just as he and Clay had rehearsed—by volunteering to stay longer to sign t-shirts and tote bags and *Spice of Life* guidebooks that had not been written by him.

He pictured Quinn signing books for the crew during the filming of her adaptation, her smile and eyes sparkling as she connected with people in her funny, demure, gracious way—basically, being her genuine self. When was the last time he had been so at home with his genuine self?

He pulled a folding chair out from the table beside the

podium and sat down, a supply of new pens with the network's logo arrayed before him on the white tablecloth. The line snaked to his left, down the length of the wall and along the back of the cavernous room, curling out the door.

Unlike Paris itself, the convention center they stuck him in was as nondescript as they came. He could be in any expo hall anywhere, and he glanced furtively at his watch trying to gauge how long it would be until he could get his ass outside, until—work obligations behind him—he could get lost in the city, until he could feel its elegance and grit, until he could smell, taste, and touch it. In his experience, you didn't so much visit Paris as absorb it through your pores.

One by one, the people in line appeared before him, some eager, some shy. He smiled and asked their name, signed whatever item they handed him, thanked them for their support, nodded goodbye.

Smile, name. Chat, sign. Thank you, bye. He enjoyed meeting them, but you had to keep the rhythm going or the talkers would never move on, and everyone still waiting in the queue got pissed.

Smile, name. Chat, sign. Thanks, bye.

His pen ran out, and he picked up a new one while still smiling and chatting, signing and thanking. He hoped he didn't look as robotic as he was starting to feel while his brain involuntarily returned to Quinn.

If she was going to the club, even if it wasn't for sex, why shouldn't he try to find a similar outlet for himself? He was in Paris, after all, sensual delights at every turn. He wouldn't be cheating since, as she kept telling him, they had no romantic relationship. What they apparently did have was a one-step-forward-and-Quinn's-defensive-walls-shoot-sky-high dance routine.

They had reached a new level of closeness with that fucking indescribable kiss, and it scared the hell out of her.

Like a song you can't stop replaying in your head, he pictured her hand rubbing his chest, the softness of her lips, the warmth of her face, the curve of her hip. No, not even a romp with a stranger in the City of Love was going to get Quinn out of his mind.

He signed his way through the rest of the line, spent some time talking with his handlers and moderators from the past few days, and as soon as it wasn't rude, bee-lined toward the door.

Out of the corner of his eye, he saw someone break away from the few last stragglers milling around the back of the room.

"Zhuh-na-tan."

He spun around at the sound of his name being spoken with that voice, that accent, that inflection. "Delphine."

"Surprise." She smiled sheepishly, rounding her shoulders, making herself momentarily smaller. The memory of how angry she had been at the shop last time he saw her stopped him from reaching out to give her a hug.

"It *is* a surprise. Are you here for the vineyard?" Perhaps the family winery had a booth in the exhibit hall or was hosting a soiree to showcase the wines, although he would have noticed that in the schedules he had memorized on the flight.

Her green eyes clouded with sadness. "Not this year."

Her father. When Jonathan had last seen her in New York, she was about to sell the shop and go back to the Jura to be with him. *He's not well.* Her face had conveyed the seriousness.

"Could we have a coffee? Do you have time?" she asked quickly.

"I do. I just finished."

"There's no fancy dinner you have to attend in a . . . What did you used to call it, your penguin suit?"

"The fancy dinner was last night." He pointed his arms straight down at his sides and waddled a few steps.

She giggled, and something in her expression told him it had been a while since she laughed. "Your humor is one reason your talk was so good. You always had that charisma." She held her hand up, her fingertips pinched together, "that *je ne sais quoi.*"

"Hah, I don't know about that, but thanks." As he spoke, they crossed an interior pedestrian walkway to a set of exit doors that faced the river Seine. "So what brings you to Paris, to the convention, if the vineyard isn't exhibiting?" Once they sat down somewhere quiet, he would ask her about Gabriel.

"I saw your photo in the paper. In an advert for the expo," she clarified fast, reminding him of that infamous photo, the one with his hand on Anna's ass while they hugged goodbye. "I was hoping we could talk."

SHE SEEMED different than when he visited her at *De Paris Avec L'amour,* her From Paris with Love shop in New York. The hard shell of resentment had softened, replaced with nervousness and, he was sad to see, pain.

They crossed the Seine over the Pont Saint-Louis bridge, hop-scotching over the two river islands, then down a few side streets and alleys to find a café free of noisy tourists and tinny renditions of "La Vie en Rose" crackling from outdoor speakers.

Outside one café, the row of marble-topped bistro tables

and woven rattan chairs was sparsely populated. He and Delphine agreed on the table at the end, beneath a tall window, its flower box filled with mums. The flowers' plum color almost matched her lipstick.

He lifted the blanket hanging over the back of the chair before pulling it out for her. Once she took a seat, he unfolded the blanket and wrapped it around her shoulders to ward off the early evening chill. He sat down across from her.

The waiter arrived, and she ordered for both of them in French: a café noisette—espresso with foamed milk—for herself and an espresso for him.

She asked about the travel convention, and soon the waiter was bringing their drinks. She held hers with both hands, but still the thermal glass cup shook slightly when she brought it to her mouth.

Something was wrong.

When she put the coffee down and rested her hands on the table, he took hold of one of them by the wrist, his palm resting on the back of her hand.

She didn't pull it away.

Now he knew for sure; something was definitely wrong.

"What's going on?" he asked. "You don't seem like yourself."

She sighed, and he suspected her demeanor was about Gabriel.

"It hasn't been so long since you and I last saw each other, but so much has changed."

"What's changed?" He prayed he was wrong. Gabriel may not have liked him, but he was a good man, and Delphine worshipped the ground he walked on.

The blanket around her shoulders slipped, and

Jonathan let go of her hand so she could pull it back up. Underneath the wool, she hugged herself.

"He passed, my father."

A sense of heaviness oozed into Jonathan's gut. He hurt for her. "I'm so sorry."

"I'm not telling you for sympathy's sake. I'm telling you because, although he was sick and we knew he was going to die, and although he has been gone for weeks, still, I forget. Something happens, or I see a thing that reminds me of him, or at the vineyard I have a question about the grapes, and I think, Papa should hear about this, Papa would know the answer, Papa would love this so I have to tell him, and then . . ."

"You remember."

Her eyes glistened, and she pulled the blanket tighter around her. "Exactly. I remember I can't tell him anymore. It's a shock, the *finalité*. A shock again and again. This is the worst part to deal with."

"You can still tell him things. You'll always be able to tell him things." He knew that was completely inadequate, but she looked so sad he had to offer something.

"I know I can, but," she laughed and sniffled while gesturing up toward the sky with her eyes, "it's not the same as having him here."

"No, it's not."

"Why I am telling you this is, after his *mort*, so many things I used to think were important became . . . petty, irrelevant. Like *bas-relief*, only a few things in one's life stand out. I was so angry at you because of what you did. But that anger is less now. It's like he took it away with him when he left. Maybe that was his gift to me, to us. Why I came here today is, I want to say I forgive you."

"Thank you," he said, holding her gaze. "I don't know that I deserve it, but thank you."

"Deserve? Who knows what we deserve? But that's the beauty of forgiveness—sometimes we get it no matter what." She sat straighter and leaned toward him, giving him the impression she felt lighter.

Maybe, like Jonathan now, she did.

The conversation flowed easier after that, less tainted by her animosity—rightful animosity—and his shame. The angle of the sun changed as it dropped toward the horizon; the breeze stilled.

"Would you like to have dinner?" he asked.

"Yes, but not here. There is a better place." She smiled.

"There is indeed. Shall we?"

"We must." He settled the bill for their coffees while she phoned the restaurant, nodding to him as she ended the call and stood. Once she re-folded the blanket and placed it over the back of her chair, he offered his arm, and she took it as they headed off side by side, the antique street lamps setting the cobblestones aglow.

PIERRE DANS LA RIVIÈRE, Stone in the River, had always been a bit rich for his tastes, but it was Delphine's favorite restaurant in Paris. With three Michelin stars, it wasn't a place you just dropped by when hunger struck, assuming you would get a table.

But when the restaurant's sommelier carried your family's special harvest wines and viewers of your former husband's travel show tripped over each other to eat at places like this, a good table miraculously opened up when you called.

Personally, he would have skipped the Stone and walked a little further down the block to the cozy neighborhood bistro, the one with the short burgundy curtains on the brass rod, the black and white tile floor, the wooden chairs and densely packed tables, the blackboard on the wall with the day's menu written in chalk. No fancy ratings, only slow, simple, salt-of-the-earth food.

He and Delphine had eaten at *Pierre* a few times, the service always impeccable, the attention too much. Tonight, as in the past, the chef came out to greet them, promised them a special meal, and excused himself to collect ingredients from the restaurant's private rooftop garden.

The meal, no surprise, was fabulous, the visual foreplay and exquisite flavors made all the more intense and memorable by how amiable he and Delphine were with each other tonight. It had been such a long time since the two of them were comfortable together.

"This is nice," she said, offering him a bite of one of the dollhouse-sized *mignardises* the chef had brought them for dessert, this particular miniature shaped like an acorn on a twig. "Us, like this."

"It is, very nice." He swirled his glass of Armagnac and held it up to her to sniff the delicate flavors.

She sniffed and tipped the glass so the amber liquid flowed close to the rim. "May I?" She gestured with her index finger.

"Sure."

She dabbed her finger in the glass and tapped it on the back of her other hand, waving it as if the droplet were perfume. A few seconds later, she sniffed the spot it had evaporated from. "Mmm. Fig."

She held her hand to his nose, and he inhaled. "Anise."

She sniffed again and nodded, impressed. He had

learned a lot about wines and spirits and haute cuisine from her. It had made him better at his job, especially as the network had begun aiming for a more upmarket, one-percenter demographic. It had helped him feel more at ease in her world.

But that was hardly a prerequisite for a good marriage.

He swirled the glass again, keeping the base warm in his hand, and inhaled the wafting aroma—notes of apricot arose this time. She was sipping a vintage Calvados that was older than she was and, note to self, he would not look at the price when he paid the bill.

"Where are you staying?" he asked when she put the glass down.

"My car is parked at the convention center. I only came for the day. I didn't think we would be so late."

The tip of her refined nose had taken on a rosy glow. It was not a good idea for her to drive. *"Fais comme chez toi,"* he said, his best French approximation of *make yourself at home.* "I was upgraded to a suite; there's plenty of room."

She held up her empty snifter. "It might be for the best."

THEY WALKED BACK to the hotel through the first arrondissement. A fine drizzle started to fall, making the cobblestones slippery. He put his arm around her shoulders as they walked along the Seine and crossed at the Pont des Arts.

Delphine. France. So foreign. So familiar.

She slowed toward the middle of the wide bridge and led them to the railing. The padlocks, thousands upon thousands placed here by lovers, had been removed, but how many romance movie scenes had been filmed where he and Delphine now stood? She put her hands on the rail and turned to him. "I never thought we would reach this day, this . . . détente."

"Me either," he answered. A lock of her hair blew in a sudden gust of wind, and he smoothed it. "But I'm happy we did. I'm only sorry your father's passing contributed."

After a few quiet minutes watching a long *bateau* sail out from under the bridge and glide down the river, they looked at each other. "Well, shall we?" he asked.

They were quiet for the rest of the walk to the hotel and through the lobby, in the elevator, and down the long red-carpeted hallway to his room.

Once inside, he helped her out of her trench coat and hung it in the closet by the door.

He poured them drinks from the minibar, a miniature bottle of cognac with a couple of ice cubes for each of them, and they sat on the couch. The ice in her glass rattled as she took off her shoes and folded her legs to the side. He sat beside her, a few inches of distance but still a chasm of disappointment, wistfulness, and caring between them.

Her forgiveness may have brought an end to her anger, but it couldn't erase history. Hurt was hurt, and it didn't just disappear. He nudged her. "He'd think you were out of your mind, your father, being here with me right now. After what happened between us."

After what I did.

She looked at him, then dropped her gaze to the glass in her hand. "Out of my mind? No. We had a lot of talks once I returned home, once we knew he would not get better. He opened up in a new way. I was so thankful for that."

Jonathan nodded and took a swig of his drink, unsure

whether he wanted to hear specifics. Her father thought, quite accurately at the time, that Jonathan was an ass.

"We were talking one day, and I asked him what he saw in you that I missed, why he was sure we wouldn't last. He told me it's what he *didn't* see in you—in us—that worried him. 'You are like friends doing business together'"—she imitated Gabriel's much deeper voice—"'and I always wished for you that you would feel passion.' That's what he told me."

"What do you think about that?" Jonathan asked her.

"I wouldn't have described it that way, but if I am honest, when I look back, he was right."

Jonathan nodded, reflecting. If he were honest, he would also have to say Gabriel was right. "I did love you." Caring, affection—that was love, too.

"I know. I did as well. I might still love you, Jonathan. But *amour* has many facets, many meanings. I was eager to live abroad, and you were my security in New York. You needed someone to make you feel like you belonged in a world you didn't grow up in. In that sense, like a lot of couples, we had an *arrangement* rather than an *amour profond*. If we were truly in love, I think you would have remained faithful. My father was right about us, but not for the reason you and I believed."

He took another swig. These weren't exactly shocking revelations, but rather straightforward observations. Accessible to anyone who could see past the bullshit story he had been telling himself long enough to notice.

You're lucky to have met a woman like this.

Don't fuck it up.

What more could you want than this?

Maybe that's what still gnawed at him so much, how cliché it was.

How *preventable*.

"These past few days, when I was deciding whether I would come to Paris to see you, I planned to ask you if you fell in love with her,"—he immediately pictured Quinn—"your girlfriend. Anna. But it doesn't matter."

"If you were wondering, it matters. I didn't, and she didn't," he answered.

With a polished fingertip, she slowly traced the rim of her glass. Her nails matched the lipstick that had worn off at dinner and, unlike the Delphine he used to know, she had not reapplied more. "I had so many questions I wanted to ask you."

"Ask me now. I promise to tell you the truth." He would, even though his stomach twisted at the thought.

"I don't need to ask anymore." She set the empty glass down on the table. "It's late," she added, standing and starting toward the suite's bedroom, then turning to look back. He followed her eyes as she stared at the sofa. "Sometimes you used to sleep on the couch when you came home late from some of your trips. Not every time. When you didn't come to bed, it was after you had seen her?"

He swallowed hard. So much for not asking questions. The truth fucking sucked. "Yes. That's right." He faced her, his arm on the back of the couch.

Each time he came home after seeing Anna, he had told himself—nice guy that he was—he would stay on the couch so he wouldn't wake Delphine. But that was bullshit. Somehow, if he waited until daylight, if he put more time between the two women, the betrayal didn't seem as egregious.

"I knew if you reached for me, if you kissed me, or wanted to make love, I would feel even more disgusted with myself," he added.

He covered his mouth with his hand and dragged it down his chin at the thought of how he had behaved back then.

He put the tumbler down on the sofa table, got up from the couch, and went to her, putting his hands on her shoulders. "I am so very sorry I hurt you, that I disrespected you like that."

"I told you, I forgive you. You don't have to apologize anymore." He watched her hand as she rubbed her neck and fingered the collar of her blouse, undoing the top button. With her other hand, she reached out and pulled him closer. "But you can show me, Zhu-na-tan. One last time, make love to me. Make love to me like I am your mistress."

EXPOSED FOR REMINDERS

In her assigned bedroom at Madame Manon's château on the outskirts of Paris, Quinn sat on the edge of the high four-poster bed, its frame elaborately carved with flowers. She guided the black stocking over her foot, careful not to nick the silk. A knock on the door made her jump; hopefully it was Octavia. "Come in," she called, adding "*entrez,*" in case it wasn't. It came out more like a question, her college French rusty from two decades of disuse.

The door opened, and Chloé slipped in. Tall and freckled, with wide green eyes and a mass of golden-red ringlets gathered atop her head, she had greeted Quinn when the car from the airport dropped her off. She explained she was Madame's full-time submissive, although Quinn could have guessed from the deferential cant of her head and her dutiful manner in Madame's presence, and the necklace, a delicate gold choker of leaves studded with ruby berries. Quinn suspected it was a collar to signify her commitment and service to Madame.

Chloé's asymmetrical chiffon dress fluttered as she extended the airy fabric in each hand and curtsied. "It is

Madame's wish to have a few words with you before dinner. I am to bring you to her when you're through dressing."

Octavia had explained that everyone was submissive to Madame at the manor.

"May I assist?" Chloé asked as Quinn adjusted the satin straps of her garter belt and clipped them to the stockings before she stood, shed her robe onto the bed, and donned the black cocktail dress she had brought from home.

Taking hold of the arm Chloé offered, she stepped into the gorgeous black stilettos borrowed from Octavia's closet before leaving New York and took her satin clutch from the nightstand. Chloé reached for something too before she joined Quinn by the gilded full-length mirror near the door. Quinn fanned her hair away from her neck, the waves falling toward her shoulders. *Don't be nervous.*

In the mirror, she saw Chloé raise the woven gold bulb of an atomizer. "Oh, no thank you," Quinn said, putting her hand up.

"It is Madame's wish," Chloé said, spritzing her with a burst of perfume.

Octavia also had warned Quinn that Madame had a sadistic side, that she would often tease her guests with unexpected acts of dominance. *Wicked* was the word Octavia had used.

In an instant, the fragrance exploded into a floral bouquet, evoking blossoms yawning open, releasing petals of color and bursts of scent. The aroma—gardenia, jasmine, others she couldn't discern—wiped away her annoyance like a drug and reminded her, as likely had been Madame's intention, that Quinn had put her trust and obedience in her hands for the weekend.

CHLOÉ WAS WAITING outside Madame's study when Quinn emerged from their meeting and ushered her to the dining room. She drew in a breath the second they walked through the tall, narrow double doors.

The room was something straight out of an architectural design magazine. Rich wood in a chevron pattern covered the floor. Carved moldings adorned the high ceiling, speckled with sculpted rosettes. At the center, from the largest floral medallion, hung the biggest, most sparkly chandelier she had ever seen.

Crystal goblets had been set out down the long table, where shining gold flatware flanked gold-trimmed plates, and silk taffeta covered the antique chairs. Panels of coordinating fabric, all bright colors and wild patterns, hung in the corners of the space like kites. Over the cavernous fireplace, swirls of intricate molding framed a mirror whose square footage rivaled some New York City studios. Well, maybe that was an exaggeration, but only slight.

She wished she had taken more art and history classes in college so she could place the period, put the room in context. But then she glanced up again at the bright taffeta sails and noticed that the carved trim along the rectangular wall panels depicted braided whips. The whimsical touches created story arcs and dynamism, a sense of change rather than a set point in time.

The other guests were beginning to gather for the evening meal, and hushed, excited conversation hummed in the background as she scanned the room for Octavia.

There she was, seated at the far end of the table, speaking with the woman next to her. The chair on her other side was empty, and Quinn headed toward it until Chloé drew her back with a hand on her elbow. "Please, allow me to show you to your seat."

It was at the opposite end of the table, on the same side as Octavia so there would be little chance of catching her eye, much less communicating, with—at rough count—fifteen or twenty people between them. Had Madame struck again, separating Quinn from the one person she knew?

She took her seat and got acquainted with the neighboring guests until Madame's arrival at the head of the table. Manon had changed outfits from when Quinn had met with her, now looking even more chic in black pants, a long black caftan, and sleek high heels. Her gray hair was pulled into a no-nonsense chignon. Quinn guessed she was in her sixties, at least. Chloé, clearly quite a bit younger, stood at her side until Madame nodded for her to take her place.

Madame toasted to an inquisitive, insightful weekend and glanced in Quinn's direction, making her tighten her clammy hold on her water glass so she wouldn't drop it. It had occurred to her that Madame might go around the table and ask her guests to introduce themselves, perhaps say something about their experience, their story, and who knew what else. Over the years giving readings and doing interviews, Quinn had mostly overcome her shyness, but in Madame Manon's home, surrounded by strangers and completely out of her depth, stress hormones surged.

Thank goodness. Madame didn't ask, and the meal began. Plate after plate—amuse bouches, a delicate salad, multiple courses of delicious bite-sized portions—a tasting menu that made dinner feel like a feast without the overindulgence.

Madame's submissives brought, placed, and cleared plates and poured water—no wine or mixed drinks—as if the meal were a synchronized ballet. At least Quinn assumed they were her submissives since each wore a choker. The women's were similar to Chloé's, only smaller, while the men wore braided black leather bands.

The food, sumptuous and flavorful, enervated Quinn's taste buds in a way she hadn't noticed since . . .

Since.

She pushed aside the vision of Jonathan cooking her dinner and the memory of his mouth on her skin as he tasted the thick, dark chocolate drops sliding down her breast.

Come *on.* How far did she have to travel to stop thinking about him, to stop remembering?

She forced herself to focus on the flavors and textures of tonight's meal. That's why she was here, to lose herself in things that weren't Jonathan or grief or the duel between longing for her old life and resisting the as-yet undefined new.

Her spoon mid-air, as she was about to take her first taste of the airy *mousse au chocolat*, Chloé touched her shoulder. "Madame wishes for you to come with me," she said, lifting the small gold utensil from Quinn's hand.

Quinn glanced around. No one else was being escorted out.

She tried to catch Octavia's eye, but that was hopeless from this distance. Besides, she was facing the other way, talking with another guest.

"Is something wrong?" Quinn whispered to Chloé. "*Quelque chose ne va pas?*"

"*Non.* Madame simply wishes for you to change for the evening's activities."

"Change?" She glanced around the table again, confirming that her black evening dress wasn't out of place. It didn't appear to be. To an outsider, this could have been a dinner among friends before heading to the opera.

"Yes. To change. It is Madame's wish."

THEY WALKED WORDLESSLY DOWN the wide hall, the sound of their footsteps muffled by the plush carpet.

Once in Quinn's room again, Chloé pointed to a rack that had not been there before. A lacy black ensemble was draped over jet-black satin hangers.

Chloé helped her change, taking her dress and turning away to hang it while Quinn undid the garter belt and replaced her underwear with a pair of beautiful black lace panties. They offered plenty of coverage in the front but left her cheeks exposed in back.

Next, Chloé helped her fasten the one-piece firmly boned corset Madame had sent and then held up a loose-sleeved black silk cover-up for Quinn to put on. She reattached the garter belt to the silk stockings, which—along with the heels she borrowed from Octavia—must have passed muster because Madame had not provided replacements.

Quinn looked in the mirror before leaving the boudoir, just like before. The lingerie was modest enough she would not be mortified and, although a tad more fabric covering her derrière would have been nice, Madame's choices gave her confidence a slight and welcome boost.

During the meeting before dinner, Madame had asked a lot of questions, and Quinn answered, sharing her limited experience at Octavia's and her brief history with Jonathan. Madame had listened intently, explained the house rules, and assured Quinn her limits would be respected. Pushed perhaps, but respected.

"Shall we go to the Great Hall now?" Chloé asked before leading her down another wide corridor, where cushioned benches and armchairs, mirrors, and potted palms lined the walls.

They entered the Great Hall through another set of tall double doors. The curved brass handles formed a horizontal letter S, sculpted in the shape of women writhing in pleasure.

Her nervousness faded as she went inside and looked around. The room was beautiful, and it helped put her at ease. Soft light from the dimmed chandeliers danced among the crystals, and candles flickered in alcoves along the moiré-covered walls. On the ceiling, a Milky Way of painted stars swirled against a midnight blue canopy, giving the illusion the space was open to the sky, that anything was possible here.

Madame sat at the far end of the space, on a platform in an ornate gold armchair, black taffeta on the carved arms, a subtle bow to the legs.

Madame's submissives—or rather, "those who give their submission," the term Madame preferred—were escorting guests, some collared and leashed, others blindfolded and bound, to couches and benches and posts, furniture that had become familiar to Quinn from Octavia's.

Chloé positioned Quinn to face Madame and stepped aside. "Madame wishes and I oblige. For your pleasure, I present Lady Q."

Madame sized her up, the path of her eyes telling Quinn she was taking in every detail.

"Simply lovely," she said, "but, devoted one"—it seemed Madame had her own lexicon—"you must breathe."

Quinn drew in a breath. "Thank you, I didn't realize—" Madame's head jerked in surprise.

"You must breathe, but you may not speak. Not without permission. If I ask you a question, you reply. If you reach your limit tonight, you may hold up your index finger, the house signal, as I explained earlier. If your hand is inaccessible to you, you may say,"—she paused, thinking—"*écrivain.*"

Writer.

"Otherwise, unless someone is experiencing a medical emergency—one that is not part of the evening's activities—you may call Chloé or me for help. Absent that unlikely scenario, you will remain silent. Do you understand?"

"Yes."

Madame nodded to Chloé, who approached Quinn and removed the lace cover-up. A chill ran through her, although the thin lace could not have been keeping her warm.

"You'll stay with me tonight," Madame told Quinn. "You want to learn? You will learn. You will be able to see everything I see." She gestured around the room.

Quinn bit her lip to keep from acknowledging the comment. Madame watched her, waiting—Quinn guessed —to see if she would answer. But Madame had not asked her a question, so she kept quiet.

"I see you understand. Marvelous. Now get to your hands and knees. Chloé will bind you."

Chloé guided her to the side of Madame's chair and helped Quinn down to a padded mat on the parquet floor. Although it was black instead of green, it still reminded her of the foam kneeling cushions she and Harris had used for gardening.

She felt Chloé slide a metal ring around her ankle and

heard it clink as Chloé fastened it to the leg of the chair. She glanced over her shoulder. No one other than Madame was behind her, but still, her ass felt like it was on display. It would be nice to have that flimsy cover-up back.

Asking was probably not a good idea.

"You'll be exposed to me for reminders about how I wish you to comport yourself this evening." By how the sound of Madame's voice moved, Quinn could tell she had turned, perhaps to reach for something.

Something that brushed across Quinn's right butt cheek, the one closest to Madame. Without thinking, she looked over her shoulder to see what it was.

Thwap! Her skin stung. *A cane?* She turned to face forward again and braced for another strike.

"As I was saying, there will be reminders." The rattan? Or birch? brushed her cheek again. A circling motion, threatening, "but you can rest assured about your limits."

"Thank . . ." *Don't speak.* The switch stung her skin again.

"And you will stay still, other than moving your head to watch what's going on in the room. I dislike fidgeting. Or squirming to get out of the path of my tools." She struck again, an underscore. "Nod once to acknowledge what I've said."

Quinn nodded once and took a deep breath to quell the burn, resisting the urge to tuck her hips. Madame dismissed Chloé.

In the dim light, Quinn sensed Madame's gaze shift to the far corner of the room, and hers naturally followed.

Before the trip, Octavia had told Quinn that Madame was one of the best in the world—"she has an ability to forge connections through all the senses," she had said. Tonight, Quinn understood. How could she, with her back turned, without any physical connection to Madame, possibly know where the woman was looking?

Somehow Madame telegraphed, and somehow Quinn received.

And now she saw what had captured Madame's attention. A dark-haired woman in a harness, with a studded black leather strap snaking down the length of her back was bent over a spanking bench, her arms stretched out in front of her, her wrists bound to a single steel loop fastened to the wood floor, her long legs held in place by a spreader bar. A man with one of Madame's leather neck bands stood behind her, his arms moving in high, rhythmic figure eights, flogging the immobilized woman with two sets of black tails.

Again and again, the fluid pattern of his movements danced in one long flowing cycle—graceful and intoxicating in its continuity.

It was only the quietest wistful sound from somewhere in Madame's throat, a sound so soft she must not have meant to emit it, that caught Quinn's attention. It was a sound that spoke to the connection between Madame and the woman, and it forced Quinn's gaze away from the man expertly wielding the whips to his subject.

Octavia.

Quinn watched, transfixed. At the club, Octavia often wore commanding outfits and thigh-high stiletto boots, boots that probably had been shined clean by her subs countless times. But this woman, who Quinn could see but not hear from her position bound to the foot of Madame's chair, was not in command. This woman had surrendered completely.

That sound Madame had let slip, it was private, protective. But Quinn heard something else in it too: longing.

She wanted so badly to turn and look at Madame's face, as if that would tell her the story of their obvious bond.

But the more she tried to stifle the urge to turn, the harder it became to stay still. And now her knee was getting sore, so she shifted the tiniest amount, just enough to relieve the weight for a second. Not even enough to slip a leaf of paper beneath it, not even enough to attract Madame's attention.

The switch struck once, twice, three . . . four . . . five times. She straightened her arms to gird herself for more, and suddenly Madame's rhythm changed. With a quick glance at Octavia again, it became clear why—Madame was striking Quinn to the same rhythm.

Her skin grew hotter from the incessant lashes, coming at a clip as fast as the two floggers striking Octavia. The sting of the cane was deep and sharp. It made her eyes water, but she didn't dare cry out or move.

Madame spoke, her voice low and commanding. "You will come with me." She snapped her fingers. "Chloé will release you."

Chloé must have been nearby because she appeared in a flash. "As Madame wishes," she said, kneeling by Quinn's leg.

Madame paused her strikes only long enough for Chloé to unfasten the cuff and step away. Quinn winced in silence, squinched her eyes and lips shut while Madame swatted her twice more and ordered her to her feet.

MADAME TAPPED THE SHIRTLESS, collared man on the shoulder. As he brought one flogger back, she took it from him without missing a beat. They lashed Octavia together, Madame's arm mirroring his serpentine motion.

She then took over the second one and nodded toward Chloé, who moved Quinn closer and whispered, her breath so close it grazed Quinn's ear, "Madame wishes for you to stand with her so she can guide you."

So she can guide what?

But Quinn went where Chloé directed and stepped in front of Madame. The rustle of her clothing against Quinn's ass made it burn even more. Madame motioned with her head and slowed her movements enough for Quinn to take hold of each handle before Madame closed her grip over the backs of Quinn's hands.

Madame piloted, showing with her own moves how Quinn should bend and snap and return her wrist, how she should strike and retreat, slice and loop her arms gracefully through the air.

Quinn's motions felt tight and jerky. "Relax your arms," Madame whispered. "And breathe. You must not stop breathing, or she will feel your tension."

Soon, Quinn's movements smoothed. Madame cued her to inhale and to exhale, to raise and lower and sweep her arm, to flick and turn her wrists. Madame didn't seem to focus on that split-second lash of leather against skin, but rather on the rhythm and pace and flow around it.

It reminded Quinn of writing. But something jarred her attention—a twitch, a shudder, some inconspicuous shift, she couldn't say what it was, only that it made her look to Octavia's face. Surely Madame had been doing so all along. The pain, not only physical, was evident, her jaw tight, her eyes not so much shut as squeezed closed in a grimace.

Breathe, she wanted to say to Octavia. *It's okay, breathe.*

Madame squeezed Quinn's hands tighter, reminding

her, warning that her shifting attention threatened to disrupt their pacing and interrupt the scene. And then Quinn saw it, how one of Octavia's shoulder blades rose a hair, how her chest caved against the bench on the other side, the teensiest bit, the subtlest sag. It was no longer willing surrender, it was something else, something Quinn could not articulate but instinctively she knew with sheer certainty. Something was troubling Octavia.

If your hand is inaccessible to you . . .

If Octavia needed to stop, she could use the safe word.

What was her safe word?

Quinn tried to remember her own. It was on the tip of her tongue but she couldn't come up with it, not with Madame's hands tightening their grip. Was she reminding Quinn to focus, or was she ratcheting up the intensity?

Octavia's wrists were sliding against one another. She was struggling against the restraint. Why wasn't she using the safe word? Maybe it rested on the tip of her tongue, too, but she couldn't remember what to say. That wasn't uncommon—Octavia herself had explained that to Quinn. That's why the club used the red, yellow, green system—it was easier to remember when you weren't fully present in your own head.

Quinn slowed her arms, overtaking Madame's considerable opposing force. "Stop," she whispered and turned to meet Madame's gaze, where fire burned.

Quinn already had broken protocol in multiple ways, and although it might mean expulsion from the manor, she added with a firmness that came from a deep sense of surety: "She. Needs. To. Stop."

Madame removed her hands from Quinn's. "Chloé will show you to your room."

She barely had to motion and Chloé appeared from the

shadows. Quinn set the floggers on a nearby table and looked at Octavia. Her back was rising and falling in rapid, shallow breaths.

"Are you . . ."

Are you okay? is what she wanted to ask Octavia as Chloé took her arm and whisked her toward the door. "Madame wishes for you to leave the Great Hall. You must come with me *immediately*."

In the doorway, Quinn paused to look back, but Chloé had anticipated that and pulled her by the arm straight out of the room.

THEY WALKED through the house in silence, Chloé only speaking once they were inside Quinn's bedroom. "I believe it will be Madame's wish to speak with you later and see to your . . ." she inhaled sharply and grimaced, "*aftercare* herself. Good night then."

Judging from the look in Madame's eyes a few moments ago, Chloé's use of *aftercare* was no doubt a euphemism.

Chloé closed the door behind her, but Quinn didn't hear footsteps. She was probably waiting right outside the door. *It is Madame's wish.*

Madame's wish my ass.

Quinn knew her role. She had submitted by coming here. But something had diverted Madame's focus. She might not have seen Octavia's worrying hands over Quinn's shoulder or noticed the subtle changes in her back or her expression, or maybe she never expected Octavia to forget a safe word.

Maybe this was a typical scene for them. It was

certainly possible Quinn had overreacted or misinterpreted the signs.

But she knew—somehow, just knew—that wasn't true.

She thought of Jonathan and how from their very first night together, although he may not have understood—how could he, when she didn't herself?—but he wouldn't have let something like this happen. He never took his eyes off her. But it wasn't only his vision; he watched her with all his senses.

At the image of him, she touched the back of her thighs, her butt. The contact stung, her fingertips finding rows of raised welts, distinct lines on an empty page.

If Madame kicked her out, the flight back to New York would be physically uncomfortable. She looked in the bathroom for some arnica cream—Octavia's was well-stocked with the salve—but there was none. She could ask Chloé, who probably had her ear glued to the door, but she was not likely to help Quinn unless *it was Madame's wish*. But Madame was pissed, so soothing cream likely was not in the offing.

She undid the corset and garters, carefully removed the stockings, and drew a lukewarm bath, the coolish water the only soothing her body was likely to get.

She had just settled in the tub when someone knocked on the bedroom door, which opened and closed before Quinn could call *come in*.

Steady footsteps tapped the floor, the bathroom door opened, and Madame walked in. "Would you like to get out and cover up?" she asked.

"It's okay," Quinn replied, then added, "but if Madame wishes."

"You are content. Stay where you are." She sat on the teak bench beside the tub, picking up Quinn's towel and draping it over the heated rod on the wall next to her. The fire in her eyes had dimmed, replaced with a trace of . . . remorse? Sadness? Quinn wished she knew her better—it was hard to get a read.

"In all the years, no one has ever interrupted me..."

"I'm very sorry. I..."

Madame broke in amid Quinn's sputtering. "Let me finish."

Quinn felt herself nod and pressed her lips together so she wouldn't interrupt Madame again.

"You were right to do so."

Madame paused, or maybe that was all she had come to say. "Is she alright?" Quinn asked. "What happened?"

"You know we don't speak of other guests. You can talk with her directly if you have questions. In the meantime, I brought you some things—a healing ointment we make ourselves and a pair of loose pajamas in silk and cashmere, the house blend, that will be cool and soft on your skin tonight. If you enjoy them, you may take them home with you when you depart."

"Depart?"

"Yes, when you leave us on Monday."

"Yes, Monday. Thank you."

"You weren't planning to move in, were you?" Finally, a small, wry grin. "There can only be one domina here, let's be clear. And we have a long wait list for those who wish to give their submission."

"No, no, I just thought you might . . ."

"Invite you to leave?"

"Well, um, yes."

"I do not like to repeat myself, but as I said, you did the right thing. You have a good instinct; in fact, maybe you'll return one day to train with me.

"But if you had *not* acted appropriately, I would have quite enjoyed inventing and delivering a suitable punishment. Much preferable to sending you away."

Quinn practically snorted. Train as a domina? Right. She pictured Jonathan and then Leigh. Each, for different reasons, would just love that. "Madame, may I ask something?"

"You may."

"Can I see her?"

Madame's *no* was clear in the silent beat. "I will tend to Tavi myself tonight. Chloé will help you prepare for bed."

Tavi? No one at the club called Octavia by a nickname.

"Thank you," Madame added as she stood to leave, "for protecting her." There was that wistful look again. Quinn wondered if perhaps Octavia had been Madame's Chloé in the past, if that's how Octavia had learned dominance—from Madame, through giving her submission.

Once Madame left and Chloé applied the house salve, Quinn put on the luxurious pajamas and climbed into bed. With one of the balcony doors open, the white curtains billowed with a gust of crisp air that brought with it a hint of woodsmoke. Nothing more than a few molecules drifting, and yet the odor held memories like two cupped hands, memories of nestling into Jonathan's side in front of the fireplace, of sleeping against him, of kissing him.

That wondrous but terrifying kiss.

Part of her wished he were here right now, lying next to her in bed. She had come here, in part, *not* to think of him. And yet, everything—everything—reminded her.

Ironically, he also was in Paris. She could get in touch. Madame collected the guests' phones upon arrival, but Quinn had gotten permission to check hers this afternoon in case Leigh or Becca had tried to reach her about the wedding reception. Maybe, since she was apparently now back in Madame's good graces, she would grant another exemption to let Quinn call him.

But why? Nothing had changed. She might want him, his body, his comfort, his . . . No. *I can't love you back.*

She reached over to turn off the bedside lamp. Hopefully Octavia was doing better and they would have a chance to talk tomorrow.

As she clicked the switch, she noticed a delicate bowl of chocolate mousse on a small plate sitting on the nightstand, the same china and gold spoon from dinner. Madame must have left dessert.

9

I DO NOT WANT A CHRISTMAS CARD

In the morning, he walked Delphine to the car park by the convention center. As they entered the garage, he asked for her ticket to see where she had left her car. She giggled, and they shared a knowing glance; her sense of direction was . . . nonexistent.

Once they found the car, they turned to face each other, and her expression grew serious. "This is a better parting than last time, but it still makes me *triste*."

He reached for her, holding her arms near the elbow. "It makes me sad also. But having this time was good for us."

"I think so too. Thank you for last night."

"Thank you for coming to Paris." Last night had brought them to a new, much better, place. Still, he had lain awake most of the night, his mind unable to settle. "Is keeping in touch a bad idea?"

"Jonathan, we were husband and wife." She took hold of his jacket lapels and shook them. "*Husband and wife*. I do not want a Christmas card from you."

"Understood."

Man, would he ever stop feeling like a heel? He leaned

in and kissed her, one cheek and then the other, and opened her car door. "Take care of yourself." He touched her back, and she looked at him one last time before she got in, started the engine, and drove away.

And now, before he spent any more dangerous time inside his own head and before he would be cooped up inside a plane for eight hours, he needed to walk.

He headed for the eighteenth arrondissement, to Montmartre, his favorite neighborhood on the right bank. It might be touristy, but it was also full of artists and picturesque, with hills and a vineyard tucked among the cobblestoned streets.

As he walked around, he thought of Delphine and last night. Sometimes he really wanted to dope slap his younger self.

Movement in a shop window caught his attention. *Stylo & Papier*, the sign said, Pen & Paper. He glanced inside the stationery store. It must have been someone walking by the window inside, but further back, standing near a table piled high with books—the profile of the woman, the curve of her neck, the chestnut color of her hair, she looked a lot like Quinn.

Reflection blurred his view through the window—people walking down the sidewalk, scooters whizzing by, the buildings behind him looming distorted in the glass. The shop window mirrored the streetscape, layer upon layer of receding images that reminded him of a Cubist painting.

But the lack of clarity was irrelevant. Of course it wasn't her, and it annoyed him that his mind would fuck with him like that. She was in New York, preparing for the wedding and—he could dream—realizing she missed him, regretting what she had said. He regretted his side of their angry conversation; his comment about using Octavia's as a grief support group was insensitive, at best. Why couldn't he have kept his pie trap shut? She had a lot to come to terms with, and, given his outburst, apparently he did too.

Now the clouds were scudding away, the sun shining down strong. Its glare ricocheted off a nearby window or car fender or some other shiny thing, obscuring his view into the shop.

But damn it—that brief thought of her made him sense her presence so strongly, like she was standing right in front of him.

He could all but feel her delicate fingers on the pages of the books in the store, examining their texture, inhaling the smell of the paper. She was so sensual. Her heart, although it was still broken and mourning, was generous, kind. The way she was helping Becca with the wedding celebration, the way she had treated everyone on the movie set—she was pretty fucking amazing.

He wanted to hear her voice. He wanted to tell her he was sorry. He wanted to tell her something else, too, but that would have to wait, who knew how long. But it was too early in New York to call without waking her.

A tap on his shoulder prompted him to turn. A mime with his face painted black and white, wearing a bowler hat, and holding a sketchpad stood behind him. The man leaned back on his heels, eyed Jonathan, and made a sequence of exaggerated faces and head tilts as if considering a palette of emotions.

He raised his marker to the pad. *Ah, got it.*

While his face moved in concentration, he sketched quickly as Jonathan stood more or less still, then made a show of putting on the finishing touches. He held it out for Jonathan to see.

It was a simple drawing. A sad man's face peered into a store window, but the reflection was smiling.

It wasn't a half-bad caricature, with its overstated bump near the bridge of the nose and the deeper dimple on one side of his mouth. But the real talent came through in the two expressions—was it that obvious to a total stranger that a split-second mind fuck, that just the *idea* of seeing Quinn, could change his demeanor from lovesick guy staring through a shop window into the reflection of a happier man?

Jonathan handed the guy a ten euro note and slid the drawing into the pocket of his laptop bag, careful not to crease it. He wanted to show it to her, evidence of how the mere thought of her made him glad.

The mime took the bill and bowed his head, *thank you*. Then he turned back toward the shop, ready for his next subject.

The bell above the shop door jingled faintly behind him as Jonathan set off to wander the neighborhood. Maybe he would take in the sweeping view of the city from Sacré-Coeur, get himself a *pain au chocolat* and a cup of strong coffee on the Square Louise Michel to clear his muddled head.

THE GAUZY CURTAINS FILTERED the morning light, softening the room's corners, and the pillowcase still smelled of lavender. The layers of mattress and feather-bedding cradled her leaden body like beach sand. She thought back to last night, on her hands and knees, bound beside Madame as she watched the scenes around the room.

Just days ago, she was unpacking boxes in a farmhouse

in New York, confirming the caterers for Becca's reception. And now she was here, in Paris, at the manor house of a world-renowned dominatrix.

It was the type of experience that, in the past, she might have imagined as part of a novel, not something that happened, at least not to her, as part of real life.

Creaking and soft footsteps from the floor above told her the house was waking up. She showered quickly and dressed, pausing only to glance in the mirror at the welts on her butt and thighs, evidence she had not dreamt this reality.

Evidence. Maybe that's why the powerful urge to see Paris had hit her this morning. She would only be here for three days; it would be a shame not to. There might not be enough time to see the Louvre, or climb the Eiffel Tower, or take a cruise along the Seine, but she could walk around, have a croissant at an outdoor café, people-watch—a brief introduction.

It occurred to her, though, that she could not simply leave the manor; she would need Madame's permission. She opened the bedroom door and peeked around the frame to find Chloé already waiting. Her expression was tired this morning, her face tight with some emotion she tried to cover with a smile. "*Bon jour*, Lady Q. How did you rest?"

"*Bon jour*. Very well, *merci*. I hope you did too." Her old French teacher would hang her head in disappointment.

"Chloé, might it be possible for me to speak with Madame for a few moments? If she wishes, of course."

"I cannot speak for Madame," she said softly, "but I would be happy to ask her."

They headed down the corridor together, stopping outside a closed door.

Quinn waited in the hall while Chloé knocked and

entered. She emerged a moment later and held the door open. "Madame wishes to see you."

She was seated on a gold chaise longue, wearing a satiny black robe with wide lace sleeves, in what Quinn guessed was the anteroom to her bedroom. The interior door was closed, and Quinn wondered if someone—*Octavia?*—was waiting for her behind it.

"*Bon jour*, devoted one. You wished to have a word?"

"Yes, Madame. Actually, there are two things. First, I wanted to ask after Octavia . . ."

"She is fine. I'll pass along your concern. Perhaps you'll see her tonight at the ball."

"I hope so." *Wrong answer.* "If Madame wishes."

She nodded approvingly. "And the second thing?"

"I was wondering—I noticed on the calendar in my room that no activities seem to be planned this morning and I would love to see a bit of Paris. Would that be okay, if I went out for a few hours?"

Quinn guessed this was not a common request, given Madame's bemused expression.

"Paris is a big place. What would you like to see?"

"I didn't really have a specific spot in mind—it's more that I'd like to walk around and . . ."

"Experience it?"

"Yes, exactly. Walk, people-watch, or if you have an area you would recommend, I would appreciate a suggestion. *If* Madame wishes," she remembered to add.

"You may go. You'll be back before lunch, which begins at one o'clock today."

"As Madame wishes. Thank you."

"I suggest you make your way to Montmartre, which is charming, and take the stairs to the top of the hill. Or," she looked at Quinn appraisingly, "if you're sore, you can take the funicular. However you get to the top, the view of Paris is spectacular. You won't have much time. Would you like us to arrange a car?"

"That's very kind, but I'd like to take the bus."

Madame gave her another approving look, followed by her devilish smile. "Chloé will return your phone temporarily, and she can explain the route. She will arrange a car to the bus stop to save you the considerable walk. But first, put out your hands."

Curious, Quinn's forehead narrowed. She extended her hands toward Madame, who turned them over, palms up, and reached beside the chaise. *A cane.* Madame had picked up her . . . *Ouch!* She struck Quinn's palms several times.

"Paris can be quite beguiling. I want you to remember why you're here."

"As Madame wishes," Quinn said, palms stinging. "I will remember."

"Marvelous. One more thing."

After the surprise caning, she didn't want to guess.

Madame got up and went to the wardrobe, but Quinn couldn't see what she removed until she settled on the chaise again.

"This goes with you—in its proper place." She handed Quinn a black lacquer box that opened like a jewelry box, revealing a small anal plug and a miniature tube of lube.

Really?

"Don't look at me like that, or I'll bend you over my knee and deliver a spanking your lovely derrière won't soon forget. And then you will have even less time in the city."

"As Madame wishes."

After a brief stop back at her room to prepare for her outing as Madame ordered—with Chloé waiting in the hall of course—she soon was on the bus, sailing along tree-lined

Parisian boulevards early on a Sunday morning, her palms hot, her ass full with the unfamiliar sensation of the plug. As the bus approached Paris proper, it slowed to navigate the old stone streets, every bump and jounce resounding inside her.

Madame was full of surprises.

When they approached the stop Chloé had indicated, Quinn signaled the driver, made her way to the door, and—gingerly—stepped off.

She crossed the street and looked around the large square. To her left, not far, was a navy awning and large wrought iron fountain pen hanging like a shingle over the door. "*Stylo & Papier*," it read. *Pen and Paper*.

The bell over the door jangled as she entered. "*Bon jour*," a clerk called in a welcoming singsong voice.

"*Bon jour*," she answered as she ambled—lumbered and hoping her discomfort wasn't obvious, was more like it—toward the postcards and gift books. A table of notebooks sat nearby, and she made her way toward them. She might not have anything in her to write, but she would never lose her love of new notebooks, their blank pages fanning open with potential.

The old wood floor creaked as she walked. Rays of sunlight shined through the shop's front window, and dust motes floated in bright tunnels. A rack squeaked as an excited little girl in a bright fuchsia jacket turned it round and round.

At the table, she picked up several notebooks, running her hands over the covers by habit, noticing how the spines gave, how they opened, whether they would lay flat so you could write to the end of the line or if they would snap closed. She felt the texture of the paper, pictured how it would hold the ink.

These kinds of details had once been important. Now, who cared if ink smudged before it dried? On what planet did it now matter if one couldn't write to the end of the line?

But maybe that's what going forward meant. Maybe, like other shifts—summer to fall, dusk to dawn—the perspective, like the light, changed.

She selected a handful of notebooks. They would make delightful gifts, perfect souvenirs from Paris. At a nearby display, she looked for a wedding card for Becca.

She and Charles seemed well suited. Quinn hoped they would be happy, that they would each feel completely seen and known by the other, like she and Harris had.

Although there was one way in which Harris didn't know her. How could he? She herself hadn't realized this part of her existed. Or maybe it hadn't existed then. Maybe it had only recently come into being. And that meant only one man knew her that way. Only one man ignited that desire.

After Chloé had left her alone last night and the house quieted, that man had taken over her thoughts. Just like he was taking them over, so strongly, right now.

Why did she have such an urge to go to him, to lean against him, to peel his clothes from his body? He was in Paris somewhere, but they might as well be worlds apart. She imagined the feel of him, the masculine, mint and leather scent of him, let it invade her senses and warm her chest and fill her with . . .

Physical need. Pure physical desire.

That's all it can ever be.

The clock hanging above the doorway ticked loudly. Her hourglass was emptying. She should get some breakfast, walk around the square. Find her way up the hill to Sacré Coeur.

When Madame mentioned climbing the stairs, Quinn had been excited for the exercise, but then Madame had gotten her bright idea for the plug and now, she decided, she would take the funicular.

And then it would be time to get back to the manor, where Madame would surely have other things in store that would help Quinn get her mind off Jonathan.

Outside the shop's tall glass windows, a street artist gestured. Black bowler hat, striped shirt, painted face, he waved his hands, sketched, then gestured again, animated by his subject. He tore a page from his pad and held it out, but the sun's brightness made her squint and the scene blurred, lost in the light and the bustling sidewalk.

She paid for the notebooks and headed out, the bells over the door tinkling.

The mime approached, sketchpad under his arm, hands in prayer pose, eyes wishful. He made a stop sign with one hand, took a pen out of his shirt pocket, and pointed it back and forth between her and the pad.

She agreed. With an exaggerated smile, he placed his hands over his heart and swayed, pretending to swoon.

He drew fast, the marker squeaking against the page he held upright so she could not see it. She pretended to peek, standing on her toes to peer over the top, eyes wide to mime curiosity.

He wagged his index finger, shook his head, and drew the pad closer.

A few more whooshes and squeaks of the pen, a couple of exaggerated, silent flourishes without the pen touching the pad, and he held it out to her.

There she was, in caricature form. Wavy dark lines of

hair, the nose with the slight off-center bump near the bridge, the same thin divot at the tip. The birthmark by the corner of her lips hadn't gone unnoticed, and he had drawn her mouth with a frown. Long lashes sprouted from wide, sad eyes. From one, a single teardrop fell.

The droplet led her gaze down the page, where he had drawn her shoulders and, beneath the left, two halves of a heart, the inner edges jagged and split. Was her melancholy so obvious?

He widened his eyes, seeking her opinion.

You got it right. She fished in her purse for the bills she had exchanged at the airport and handed him a few. He shook his head no, gave them back, and mimed wiping an invisible tear from her cheek. His hands formed the prayer pose again, and she understood: *Don't be sad.*

10

VOLATILE AND EPHEMERAL

All afternoon, the manor house perked with energy in anticipation of tonight's event—a ball, the calendar said. Madame's submissives toted wood beams, power tools, and duffle bags to the Great Hall and up the wide white limestone stairs to the Upper Hall.

A two-story event. And what did it say about her plans that there was construction?

Before dinner, Chloé came to Quinn's room and placed a box on the dresser. "Madame wishes for you to have this. She wishes for your body to be free of tension this evening, so you should use the contents to achieve *la petite mort*. Afterward, she wishes for you to remove the gift she gave you earlier. When you've carried out Madame's wishes, knock on your door and I'll return."

When Chloé left, Quinn opened the box. Lined with sapphire velvet, it held an array of toys. Quinn selected one with an S-shaped, come-hither curve, crawled onto the bed, and slipped the toy under her robe. This time, she needed none of the lube that the box also held.

Wearing the plug had been new, and at times uncomfortable, like when she got back on the bus to return to the manor. But when thoughts of Jonathan intruded—imagining him finding her with it inside her, picturing what he would do to her while she wore it—they brought her arousal level unexpectedly high.

The toy slid smoothly, and she seated it deep. *Breathe,* she imagined him saying. She turned it on and the curved surface began stroking its mark, and each time she shifted her hips in time with its movements, the plug stroked her from behind.

Breathe. That's what he would tell her, or he would press her hip to still her motion. *Shh, not yet,* he would say, and she would melt a little more.

The harder she tried not to picture him, the clearer the fantasy grew—him behind her, him inside her, his arms tightly around her while he thrust. He bore into her slow and deep, teased her earlobe with his teeth, traced the line of her neck with his tongue, bit her shoulder hard to delay his climax until she reached her own.

She stifled her cry in the duvet as her muscles clenched and relaxed in their familiar dance. The intensity had been building all day, but it was fantasizing about him that triggered this shuddering release.

So much for Madame's diversions that would help her forget, so much for the *petite mort* to free her from stress.

After she cleaned up and put the toys away, and waited for the blush to leave her face, she alerted Chloé, who came in and headed for the bathroom.

"Madame wishes that I draw you a bath and help you dress for this evening," she called back.

After the bath, she asked Quinn to sit at the vanity so she could work on her hair.

The pointed end of the comb Chloé used to section her

hair tickled her scalp, every part of her hyperaware with curiosity about what Madame had planned.

Chloé wove one braid and wrapped it into a small, tight bun high on her head. "Madame requires your hair up tonight."

Next Chloé helped her into the outfit Madame had sent: a magnificent floor-length black gown, with a neckline that plunged beyond the hollow between her breasts. Two feather-light straps met at the back of her neck, and Chloé tied them into a bow.

She met Quinn's eyes in the mirror. "You will not wear panties or stockings or jewelry, and you must not use any lotions, creams, or *parfum*. You may not add products to your hair. These are not only Madame's wishes but strict requirements for everyone's safety. Madame wishes for you to confirm you will comply."

"Yes, of course. As Madame wishes."

She scanned her memory for the scenes she had witnessed around the Great Hall last night, but couldn't recall any that warranted such precautions.

"But, may I ask, why?"

Chloé smiled and pursed her lips. "Lady Q, do you think Madame would wish for me to tell you?"

TWO SHIRTLESS MEN in eye masks, black collars, and tight black pants flanked the entrance to the Upper Hall, faces rapt with concentration as they shot blazes straight up into the air from handheld flamethrowers while guests entered the room.

Once everyone was inside, Madame followed. "*Bienv-enue, dévoués*," she said loudly, gesturing to the black ceiling. The men shot three more bursts of flame, and Quinn followed their flight upward. Each ignited a word suspended in darkness: *Ball of Fire.*

The guests broke into applause, and Madame ushered them deeper into the room. Flares erupted throughout the immense space, timed with the flickering of antique Parisian street lights, paired in a long row down the center of the room to create an indoor boulevard.

Quinn looked around at the other guests. A few wore fetish wear, others costumes with elaborate masks—a leopard, a butterfly, a peacock—trimmed in gold, flush with feather plumes. They gathered in small groups or stood alone, like she was, staring up in wonder.

Swirls of flame shot into the air from tall square stanchions, while fire-eaters stood on raised triangular platforms built into the corners, blowing kisses of fire. Closer to the center, large wrought iron rings hung from the ceiling, a woman perched atop each one, sending down whooshing blazes safely above the heads of Madame's guests. Choreographed flame and heat, dazzling light, and barely contained danger.

Her upper lip and the dip of her breastbone where the silk touched her body grew moist in the warm, electrified air. Her skin prickled with anxiety.

She looked around for Octavia, who was talking to Madame, her trusty cane in hand. Octavia's hair was also in an updo, her dress also sleeve- and backless. Quinn couldn't hear them at this distance, but the tension near Octavia's eyes told her the two women were not in agreement.

Octavia turned, caught sight of Quinn, and waved while Madame's expression changed, almost imperceptibly, from confidence to something else. Sadness? A tinge of fear? The change might be subtle, but from a distance, with visual cues Quinn's only input, it was clear. Like how when one sense falters, another compensates, like how when Jonathan blindfolded her, the sound of his breathing and the feel of his body intensified.

Not thinking of him tonight.

Octavia was coming toward her now. "Finally," Quinn said with a relieved sigh. "How are you doing?"

"I'm fine," although the drop of her gaze made Quinn question how fine. "I should ask you that question—I thought we would have more time to talk."

"It's a little, um . . . intense," Quinn said.

"I hope not too intense." Octavia's eyes added a question mark.

"No. But definitely out of the comfort zone." Quinn was about to ask her about last night, but stopped short when she noticed Madame coming to join them.

"I trust you followed the instructions Chloé delivered?" she asked Quinn.

"Yes, as Madame wished."

"Wonderful." She looked from Quinn to Octavia and back. "I thought we'd explore something different tonight."

"Yes, of course—as Madame wishes," she answered before the realization struck: *Fire.*

Her mouth went dry as sand and, a split-second later, her ass stung. Damn it, that wicked cane.

"I didn't ask a question. But I do appreciate your openness."

Quinn kept her mouth shut while Madame reminded her of the safe word and signal and then gestured over her shoulder. Two collared men appeared on either side of Quinn. Without a word, they took her by the elbows and led her away.

Other guests turned to watch as the men took her down

the lamp-lined boulevard. Like last night, she was the only one being removed.

They brought her to a side room, and one of the men opened the door. The other directed her through and closed it once the three of them were inside.

It was dark, the only light coming from the gap between the floor and the bottom of the door. As her eyes adjusted, she made out a metal table in the center. They helped her onto it, guided her so she was on her belly, her cheek on the cold, hard surface. And then, without a word, they left her alone.

A beat or two after the door shut, the line of light went out. They must have put something there to cover the space.

A shiver of anxiety chilled her, and she rolled onto her side so she could cross her arms and rub them. The sound of her palms against her skin, of shallow breaths, of her pulse thudding in her ear were all she could hear despite the activity in the Upper Hall.

Nothing happened for a long time. Or only a few minutes. The silence, the pitch dark, the isolation, they made it hard to know.

But then, the door opened, and people filed in. During the brief moment of light, she could make out Octavia along with the two men, who donned black hoods that reached to their shoulders and revealed only their eyes.

Madame must have come in as well, because now she stood beside Quinn and helped her roll onto her stomach. She untied the top of Quinn's dress at her neck, and the straps fell loose onto the table. A dagger of fear ran through her.

"Tavi is going to move the top of your dress out of the way," Madame said. Octavia appeared beside Madame and tugged the two front pieces of fabric down with one hand on either side of Quinn's body, then tucked them under Quinn's thighs. Octavia rolled the waistband down too and tucked in some kind of light, crinkly material—*foil?*—so it covered the lowest part of Quinn's back and her buttocks. Then she turned toward the counter at the end of the room to do something, although Quinn couldn't see what it was.

"You won't be restrained," Madame told her. "That's one of our fire rules, but you must stay completely still. Do you understand?"

Another stab of fear jolted her.

"As Madame wishes," Quinn eked, turning her head toward the woman's voice.

"Completely still," Madame repeated, pressing on the back of Quinn's head for emphasis.

Octavia was there again, moving something soft and ice cold down the center of her back. The smell invaded her nostrils and chilled the back of her throat. *Cotton dipped in alcohol?* There was a click, the sound of a flint, and a surge of air heated her back, a dragon exhaling fire.

Panic rose in her chest, and the flood of adrenaline set off a primal instinct to jump up and run.

Two pairs of hands pressed on her shoulders and arms. "Stay still," Octavia whispered, as heat hovered above Quinn's back, close but not touching. Like a warm body was lying behind her.

A particular warm body.

She tried to make the unwelcome thought of Jonathan go away by focusing on how the heat moved above her back, how the warmth radiated, how it relaxed her skin, her muscles, her bones.

Until Madame dripped something—a melting ice cube? —along the same path. The icy drops fell into the crook of her collarbone, jarring, and begged to be wiped away. But

Madame held Quinn's arm in place—whether for safety or because, as Octavia had said, she had a sadistic streak, Quinn didn't know.

What she did know was that the frigid drops tickled her back in places she could not reach, and it was starting to piss her off.

Along Quinn's spine, Octavia dragged another icy glacier, bringing a fresh wisp of alcohol fumes.

There was the *ffftt* of the flint, and as the primal fear was about to peak again, the heat descended.

They repeated the sequence again and again. One man always had his palm flat at the base of her spine, where the foil blanket covered her dress and met her skin. Just in case the dragon's breath didn't extinguish on its own, she knew he would reinforce the boundary and protect her.

Wild, tame. Danger, safety.

She lost count of how many times they began anew, igniting fire from a thin strip of cold fuel, volatile and ephemeral, flaming out before it burned. Each cycle took only a few seconds, but it was long enough: Each bolt of fear and lick of flame extinguished into a calming, hypnotic heat.

They were moving around the room now. She wanted to see what they were doing, but a sense of heaviness kept her eyes closed, kept her body still. It was easier now not to move, to let the tightness release.

To surrender.

One of the men stepped back, and the smell of alcohol filled her nostrils again. There was that familiar whoosh and warm flare and then an unfamiliar thump to one side of her back. A second thud on the other side followed, and a third, on the first side.

Each whump rumbled deep, a drumbeat of heat and reverberation.

The sensations kept her weighted, flat against the table, tethered to physicality. There was no space in the heat to hold thoughts or feelings, memory, or expectation.

The way the man moved, the way the heat flowed, she could tell he was drumming figure-eights, raising the fiery wand, thumping. A pattern similar to the one she and Madame had used with Octavia last night.

The warm vibration rocked her body—her skin, her core. The drubbing resounded deep, shaking something loose that was so small, so subtle, she could not find words for it.

Eventually he slowed his dancing arms to a stop. The wands gave off a hint of smoke—he must have extinguished them. Soon, there was more shuffling, the gathering of things, hushed voices. The door opened and closed.

Her eyelids heavy, she kept them shut even when Madame spoke. "That was magnificent. Tavi will see to your care tonight."

She sensed Madame step away and pictured her wistful expression as she added, "She insists." Quinn heard her footsteps move toward the door.

"You did great," Octavia whispered as she pressed a cool, moist cloth to Quinn's damp forehead. "How do you feel?"

Quinn nodded to signal she was fine. But she wasn't yet ready to talk, her body heavy, her mind light and deliriously free.

The thoughts, the sadness, the fears, the missing—they all hovered at the edge of consciousness, but that's where they stayed. As if the white heat from the blazing wands had opposed them, a force to keep them away.

THE BEDSIDE LAMP in Quinn's room had been switched on while she attended the ball; the bed's soft duvet had been turned down, pillows fluffed. While she washed her face, Octavia leaned on the bathroom doorframe, waiting to help her change out of her dress and into the cool satiny pajamas someone had left neatly folded on the counter. Quinn pictured Chloé, efficient, nymph-like, preparing the room.

As Quinn climbed into the high bed, Octavia let her know Madame had sent a new jar of cream. "I'll put it on you if you like."

"That would be wonderful." Her back didn't hurt, but her skin felt like she had been at the beach, massaged by the sand and fine salt and sun. "Are there any marks?" She pictured her dress for the wedding, with its low cowl neck in the front and in the back.

"No marks," Octavia said as Quinn rolled onto her stomach. "Madame likes fire play because of its potential— the closeness to the heat and the flame, the complete submission to the top who has *so* much responsibility and control. That potential is part of what takes you to the edge."

Octavia sat on the bed beside Quinn and picked up the jar from the nightstand. "There's always risk, that's why she takes so many precautions. Us, too. At the club, the fire room checklist is almost fifty steps long. Is it okay if I turn the sheet down and lift your top?"

Quinn agreed and soon the air filled with the floral scent of the cream as Octavia rubbed it into her back.

"She thinks of everything, doesn't she?" Quinn asked, turning her head and resting it on the back of her hands.

"Every. Single. Detail. I'm glad you could experience it —to experience her—for yourself."

"It's like a fantasy world, every single thing attended to."

"She has this uncanny way of knowing what each person needs, and she creates it for them. I used to tease her that she's less of a sadist than she likes to believe."

Quinn nodded, taking it in.

Madame had chosen fire play for her. She recalled all the months after Harris, the bone-deep chill she could not shake, her soul frozen. She hadn't shared that with Madame. What she had voiced was how she had come here to stop thinking of Jonathan, to let him go because she could not accept what was growing between them.

Ironically, though, he had not stopped taking center stage in her mind's eye all weekend. And then she recalled how Madame missed the signs with Octavia last night. What had Madame believed Octavia needed, and why had she let the delivery go too far? Maybe her magic cane was broken, or perhaps she was losing her touch, or was it that emotion had clouded her view?

Quinn's skin hummed, the salve like a cool breeze rippling across a lake, Octavia's soothing hands a stabilizing force that dissipated the waves.

There was something intangible in Octavia's touch, the way the heel of her hand kneaded Quinn's back, in her long, comforting strokes, in the tenderness that brought tears to Quinn's eyes. She felt protected and safe, almost as safe as when she was with . . .

Damn it. A few tears slid across the bridge of her nose, tickling her skin, and she wiped them away.

Maybe Octavia wouldn't notice, but even in the low light she did. "It's totally normal to get emotional," she whispered, pausing to tug a tissue out of the box on the night table and put it in Quinn's hand. "If you want to talk, I'm here." She went back to rubbing Quinn's back in a circular motion. "I'm right here."

Quinn sniffled and nodded. She had seen many people cry at the club after their scenes, the release could be that powerful.

"Even though it might not seem like it, tonight was a lot," Octavia said after a few minutes of quiet, the only sounds the shushing of her hand on Quinn's skin and the occasional footfall in the hallway. "It would have been a lot for someone with more experience. Madame pushed you hard. Your sensitivity, your sensuality, your curiosity—you feel so keenly. It makes you well suited to the lifestyle, but it also has consequences."

"Great. The whole point was *not* to feel."

"Good luck with that." Her gentle laughter shaded the edges of the words like a soft charcoal pencil. She paused for a couple of seconds, seeming unsure if she should say more, and then went on. "I suspect it comes from what you've gone through, from mourning such a significant loss. You've been laid bare, broken open. It gives you this . . . raw vulnerability, without being weak. Quite the opposite, in fact."

Octavia was right in a sense. The life Quinn knew had been stripped away; there was nothing left to hide behind. Maybe that's why she had needed distance between her and Jonathan, why she had built up scar tissue around her heart.

"That rawness, it brings out a protective instinct in some people," Octavia said.

Quinn turned her head to look at her, one teary eye cocked. "You're not referring to anyone in particular, are you?"

Octavia let out a guilty laugh. "Okay, busted. Subtlety may not be my greatest asset." She stopped rubbing Quinn's back, covered her with the sheet, then swung her legs onto the bed and wrapped her arms around her bent knees.

"He wants to care for you."

You could let him.

"It makes me queasy to think about. I can't—"

"—accept that you have those feelings?" Octavia drew the sheet further up to Quinn's shoulders and tucked it around her. When she shivered, Octavia covered her with the down duvet.

"It just seems safer without all of that in my life." She stuck her hand out in front of her, as if fending off something dangerous. Better to stick with the narrative. *Grieving widow, can't risk more pain.* Full stop.

"For now, it may seem safer. But I can imagine there might come a time when that starts to change," Octavia said, scissoring her index and middle finger to signify reversal. "When letting him in will feel less threatening."

"It's so hard to imagine having that kind of relationship again."

"I know," Octavia whispered, her hand on Quinn's shoulder. "Trust me, I do. But you don't have to make any decisions or do anything about it tonight."

Maybe it was the deep heat of the fire that made the hardened emotions soften like melting wax, until it was impossible to deny the truth: She missed Jonathan like mad, and she did not want to keep pushing him away.

But the fog of sleep rolled in, and she yawned. "I'll stay with you tonight," Octavia said softly, "I'll sleep on the chaise."

"That's alright, you should go to Madame," Quinn murmured. She wanted to ask Octavia what happened between the two of them last night—maybe Octavia needed to talk, too. But besides succumbing to sleep, she realized this conversation would be better to have once they were back in New York, when Octavia had more distance. "You can tell her I'm fine."

"Madame didn't ask me to stay with you—I want to."

In the past, Quinn would have brushed aside the offer more strongly a second time, but Octavia was so comforting. Like a skilled therapist, masseuse, and funny, wise friend, all rolled into one. Maybe she was right; maybe it was time to let in people who cared and wanted to help.

"The bed's huge; sleep here," Quinn said, gesturing toward the expanse of untouched mattress. "And thank you. For inviting me here. For everything. There's no one else I can talk to about any of this."

"Don't thank me. I understand." Still sitting near the edge of the bed, Octavia began rubbing Quinn's back again, light and slow over the bedding. "I know what it's like to keep something that's important to you—something important *about* you—to yourself. Those secrets can start to weigh heavy."

Octavia continued to rub her back until Quinn's thoughts of Jonathan—tomorrow; she would call him tomorrow—faded into slumber.

THE CAR MADAME summoned to take Quinn to the airport traveled down the winding driveway away from the manor. Like a character emerging from a fantastical world, she watched the rearview mirror as the stately white mansion and its manicured gardens shrunk in the growing distance.

Madame Manon's *was* another world, one of fantasy and reality, need and fulfillment, freedom and responsibility. She had emphasized again and again that what happened at the manor stayed at the manor, just like at Octavia's. Many members of the club had precious things at stake.

The sedan cruised along the highway to Charles de Gaulle Airport. How strange that Jonathan also had been here in Paris and yet their immediate surroundings, their purposes, were so different.

She wanted to tell him about the weekend with Madame. Not about the *who*—she would never disclose any of that, not even to him—but about the *what*, what she had experienced here. He had told her he didn't understand, but still, she wanted to see him, to have him next to her, look into his eyes and tell him. The anger and hurt and fear that had gripped, white-knuckled, somehow now eluded her.

She looked between the front seats at the dashboard clock. Subtract six hours for the time difference and it was too early in New York to call, but she would as soon as she landed. It might be awkward at first, and . . . well, so what?

She would tell him she needed to see him; she would tell him she missed him. They each had issues to work through. She needed to open up to him more than physically, to put her heart on the line again, and he would have to come to terms with her being part of the lifestyle and going to the club. But too much had developed between them these past months not to try.

To take a small step. A next step.

She pictured him walking into the barn for Becca's wedding and how her heart would pound at the sight of him, natty and debonair in his tux, how her hands would grow damp, her mouth dry. Even with tension between them, his smile would tug at the corners of his eyes, and his touch would be gentle when he hugged her. And she would lean against him, inhale his scent, and find herself lighter and happier simply because he was close.

There, she had a plan: She would call once the plane touched down, when it would be late morning in New York. She could take a cab straight into the city to see him. Later, they could have a quiet dinner, order something in, sit together on his couch and . . . The car pulled up to the entrance for her airline and the driver got out, opened her door, and offered his hand to help.

She glanced at the meter, which hadn't moved. Madame had paid. Quinn tipped the man generously, took the handle of her roller bag from him, said thank you, and headed inside.

Once past security, she ducked into a shop along the concourse to the gate to pick up chewing gum and a magazine. The newspapers on a rack at the entrance stopped her cold. The top shelf, tilted like a music stand for easy reading, held three colorful tabloids, each with grainy photos of a man she knew.

But not all the photos were of Jonathan.

A zoomed-in photo of his head also showed a woman's, presumably the two of them moving apart after a kiss. The headline in big block letters asked, *"Can this frequent-flier be trusted now?"*

The headline of the second cover posed a different question: *"Rough night, mate?"* It hung over a photo of Jonathan on the sidewalk in front of a hotel, its sign easily decipherable. The photographer had caught him with bed head, shoulders hunched, hands stuffed in his front pockets, classic walk of shame posture.

The third cover led with, *"Romantic Paris reunion. Will it last?"*

She must have possessed an anatomic structure not yet

known to science, because it felt like a trapdoor between her chest and her stomach gave way. That third cover was the hardest to look at. The way he held the woman beside him —Delphine, she assumed from the headlines—his arm over her shoulders, his fingers curled around her bicep in a fully-engaged hold. The way his head canted as he looked at her. The way they gazed at each other.

The photos . . . She felt lightheaded. Her hand shook as she picked up one of the papers, opened to the story, and scanned the article.

Wait, why was she doing this? The details didn't matter. In fact, she should be relieved. No more angst or pressure to move forward, no need to take that risk. No need to worry she would disappoint or hurt him. He belonged to someone else. She should be happy for him. He had wanted Delphine's forgiveness, and it was obvious from these photos he had gotten it.

And no doubt a whole lot more.

11

SOME FAKE RELATIONSHIP THING

As soon as he cleared customs, he put his sunglasses on and headed to the nearest set of sliding doors. Gil was waiting outside with the car, smoke drifting from the open driver's window. The cool morning air was moist with dew, the sun low but already bright. Even with the glasses, the light stabbed his jetlagged eyeballs.

Gil looked at him sympathetically in the rearview mirror. "To the apartment or the office or—"

"Office. If I go home, the day will be a goner." It was all but guaranteed: He would sit on the couch and half-heartedly check email, then lie down to get more comfortable before opening a few envelopes plucked from the waiting stack of mail. Next thing he knew, he'd snore himself awake in four or five hours, his throat dry, neck aching from using the armrest as a pillow, his sense of time all fucked up, insomnia ready to dog him the whole damn night. And he would spend that whole sleepless night thinking—no, ruminating—about Quinn.

It was much better to go to work, take a walk in the park

over lunch, and keep his sorry ass awake for the next four-teen hours.

Out of habit, he pulled his phone out of the side pocket of his bag but quickly remembered the battery had croaked during the flight, so he stuck it back in.

Gil parallel parked in front of the network's office tower, and Jonathan patted his shoulder before Gil could jump out to open the door. "Don't bother, man. Thanks for the ride." He hated Gil waiting on him; formality was not his style.

As the elevator opened onto his floor, Mike traipsed by. The tip of his loosened tie swayed in the air current he kicked up. "You're back."

Nice to see you too, asshole.

It was early, but the undone tie and the unfastened top buttons of his burgundy dress shirt told Jonathan his morning was not off to a great start.

Which meant Jonathan's would not be either.

"Yeah, I'm ba—"

"Lost your phone?"

He patted the pouch to check. "No, it's right—"

"Getting coffee. Meet in my office."

What crawled up his ass while Jonathan was away?

He continued down the hall to Mike's office and sat in one of the two guest chairs, modern ones with a thin steel frame and some exotic animal skin slung across it for a seat. The poor beast was probably poached, if Mike had anything to do with procuring it.

Jonathan hadn't been in the wildebeest sling for more than a minute when Mike returned, the cup mostly drained. Mike with a caffeine buzz—things could get ugly.

"Congratulations," he said, sitting on his desk and

crossing his arms, the instant height disparity a common Mike power pose that no longer intimidated him.

"Yeah, thanks, the expo went well—two sold-out talks, signed a lot of books, sold out the meet-and-greets, did three trade interviews . . ."

"I meant Delphine. Looks like it was a joyful reunion."

"Yeah, it was a good visit . . ." Whoa, why was Mike talking about Delphine?

"Are you shittin me, J.J.? Tell me you didn't see it."

"Guess I didn't see *it* because I don't know what you're talking about."

Mike picked up a tablet from his desk, snaked and tapped his stubby finger around the screen and thrust it toward him.

The tiled browser windows showed the home pages of three Paris tabloids. Jonathan scanned the screen and saw the headline, its English translation roughly, *"Can this frequent-flier be trusted?"* The blurry photo showed him moving away from Delphine. He could see from the grainy background where the shot was taken—right by the foot of the bridge they crossed on their way to dinner. It had been crowded and noisy, and he had leaned close to say something. He had to hand it to the photographer, who captured a nanosecond in time that made it appear as though they just kissed.

The second browser window showed an image of him walking alone, outside a hotel. It wasn't even the hotel he stayed at. *"Rough night, mate?"* This photog had caught a posture and facial expression that made him look like a skulking jerk, like the kind of guy who might, for example, have cheated on his wife.

He didn't bother reading the last one.

"It must have been a slow news day, but they did it

again." He rubbed his forehead. At least this time, he wasn't cheating on her. "My phone died mid-flight. I didn't see any of it."

"I talked to Maddie earlier, and this time we're going to channel the attention. It ain't gonna wag us around like a bunch of lap-dog pussies—Maddie didn't say pussies—the way it did last time."

Great. Maddie—Maddox Winstone—was the network president, the same one who made her displeasure clear after his previous dustup. Jonathan tried to fly well under her radar.

"J.J., you listening? Here's what we're thinking—" Mike looked at him over the rim of the mug and took a slurp of coffee. "They're interested in your love life, we'll give em your love life."

If Jonathan had been the one drinking, coffee would have sprayed from his nostrils. "*What* love life, Mike? Nothing happened." But even as he said it, he knew how it looked. Who gave a shit about the truth when there was more drama and money around the fiction?

"It doesn't matter. You know these sleaze-hounds, it doesn't matter. So we bring a woman onto the show to give you a love life."

Great, so Mike and Maddie had cooked up some fake relationship thing. Just what he needed.

"But not *any* woman," Mike added dramatically.

"Okay . . . Who?"

Mike looked at him. "Hel-lo-oh. Delphine."

"Delphine?"

"Delphine. Now that we're clear on your wife's name." He shook his head at Jonathan's obvious stupidity. "It's genius."

"Ex-wife." *How is that genius?*

"Even better. Think about it: She's younger. She's pretty. She has an endearing accent. She's rich. She's French. She's rich. Need I go on?"

"I know, she's great, but . . ."

"She doesn't have to be in every episode, but we tie her in. You two video chat, send some racy texts, you share some of the material with her you would otherwise have narrated. You say goodbye to her when you leave for a trip and kiss her when you come back. Every few episodes, she goes with you. You have spats; you make up. She's the chic, old money French sophisticate to your . . . to your . . . to you." Mike stumbled, not sure how to describe Jonathan's TV persona, the one the network had watered down to nothing discernible. "It's absolutely brilliant."

"I'm not sure that's how I'd describe it."

"It's original, and that's what we're after."

I gave you original.

"She would never agree." Actually, he would never ask; he had disrupted her life enough already. "And you're talking about a whole different show."

This must be a pilot episode for some hidden-camera reality show with a "gotcha" moment that Mike was about to spring on him—the idea was that absurd.

Mike walked his feet back a couple of steps so he sat taller, put the coffee cup down on a legal pad that already sported several brown rings, and jerked his tie knot even looser. "Look. You haven't made it easy. You got caught having an embarrassing affair. We kept you on, paid out the ass to that PR firm to bury as much as we could. Now, it's reared its head again, and we're going to leverage it. We sell expensive advertising to top-tier global brands, J.J., we don't give away tote bags and DVDs when someone sends us fifty bucks. Your fuckfest in Paris gave us an opportunity. Your show may be decent, but it's overdue for a makeover."

The way Jonathan saw it, they already had been making over his show. "Wow. Why haven't we discussed this before?"

"We have. Just not with you in the room. This thing with your wife, ex-wife, whatever, it validated what Clay's been saying about needing a change."

Jonathan pushed off the gazelle pelt and stood. Now he was taller than Mike, Mike who had no scriptwriting or development or production experience to speak of. "Clay didn't create the show. I did." He was thumping his chest with his thumb like some baboon. That's the effect Mike seemed to have on him lately. "It would be nice to be included in the conversation."

"But he made the show profitable, J.J.—very profitable— which trumps your creative vision." He rocked his shoulders mockingly when he said "creative vision" like Jonathan must fancy himself an artiste.

"I appreciate all the support. I can tell you're really going to the mat for me." *Asshole.*

"Think about it, J.J. Talk to Delphine. Clay and I meet with Maddie again Wednesday." He squeezed past Jonathan and sat in his desk chair. "You can join us."

Nice. A condescending last-minute invite to his rightful seat at the table.

"By the way, you remember the awards are next Friday, right?"

The Compass Awards. "Yeah." A long evening of fake smiling in a dark auditorium with your ass falling asleep in your seat. To ease the pain, he had planned to ask Quinn to join him at the ceremony, but he left abruptly last time they were together and now, well, they weren't exactly on speaking terms.

Besides, she probably would be busy at the club. Not to mention that with the Delphine photos, bringing anyone else but her would make him appear guilty of cheating. Again.

"Good. Be ready with a brief speech, two minutes, and don't forget anyone on the thank-yous."

"You're telling me how badly the show needs a makeover, and we're winning something?" Hope flickered.

Mike gave him a funny look. Jonathan knew he couldn't divulge more—executives were sworn to secrecy. The ceremony was the network's annual attention-seeking event. He pictured the usual stage fireworks, the sparkling gowns and tuxes, the schmoozing and ass-kissing of entertainment journalists and advertisers, the carbon-puffing limos up the wazoo.

But Mike just asked him for a brief speech. Despite what he said about *Spice of Life*'s future direction, maybe, just maybe, Jonathan's show would finally be recognized.

12

NEXT?

Quinn shifted the bouquet of deep purple calla lilies so she could knock on the doorframe of Octavia's suite at the club. Her "come in" was muffled and the darkness, unexpected.

"I just stopped by to bring you these"—Quinn held out the flowers haltingly—"but are you *okay?*" It took a second for her eyes to adjust.

When they landed on Octavia, she was flat on the couch under one of the club's soft black blankets with the embroidered script burgundy O. Quinn took a couple of steps to see better. Octavia's eyelids were puffy, the tip of her nose chafed. A box of tissues sat on the table along with a miniature city skyline of cold medicines and nose sprays.

"Define okay," Octavia deadpanned in a hoarse voice, then promptly sneezed. "Stand back. I don't know what I caught between Charles de Gaulle and JFK, but trust me, you don't want it. Why flowers?"

"To say thank you again for inviting me to Madame's. It really was a once-in-a-lifetime experience."

"It was a pleasure to share it with someone so curious and receptive. It can get, as you put it, intense. Madame was delighted to have you there."

With her congestion, Octavia's "there" sounded like "air," which clearly she wasn't getting enough of. She reached for a tissue just in time to catch another sneeze.

"Why aren't you home in bed?"

"It wasn't this bad when I came in this afternoon." She sat up slowly, and now Quinn could see that fever glazed her eyes.

"You shouldn't be at work. Let me take you home."

"I can rest here. I don't want to leave Alex by himself. We're shorthanded tonight, again."

Octavia was exceedingly careful with hiring, and the club's vetting and training program was long, which meant there wasn't exactly an overabundance of qualified substitutes to cover in a pinch.

"Can I work with Alex? I know I'm not trained, but I know the confidentiality rules; Alex can tell me what to do; and I can call you if we need help—that way, at least he won't be alone."

Octavia looked at her. One eye watered, and she dabbed it with the tissue in her hand. "You may have to monitor level three if the club gets more crowded and he's busy on the main floor. Are you comfortable with that?"

"I can handle it. I'm wearing my big-girl undies today." Quinn pretended to tug with her thumbs at a high, imaginary waistband.

Octavia's laugh turned into a coughing fit. "Okay," she rasped, reaching for the nearby glass and taking a sip. She pointed toward the closet, toward the racks of costumes, lingerie, and kinky outfits Quinn had borrowed from before. "Help yourself. And actually, this is a great opportunity for you to sit on the other side of the desk, so to speak. Maximillian booked the fire room. He's a trained fire top, and he brings his own spotters. If Alex isn't busy, you should join them as long as it's okay with Maximillian and his sub. You'll learn a lot."

THE FIRE ROOM at Octavia's was smaller than at Madame Manon's château. Maximillian stood beside his sub, who lay prone on the table, with nothing but a foil blanket beneath her. One spotter stood by her head, her hair also up and off her neck, while the other stood across from Maximillian. Overhead, a petite chandelier cast a diffuse glow, each drape of pea-sized crystals delicate enough for a necklace. It was a signature Octavia touch, subtle elegance in a room where other decoration posed a risk.

Quinn leaned against the countertop along the far wall, as much out of the way as she could get. Beside her sat a fire extinguisher and a metal bucket of water, a pile of neatly folded wool blankets, and, mounted to the wall, a first aid kit, a red canvas pouch labeled *fire blanket*, and a telephone. Next to it hung a laminated list of emergency numbers in large print.

Maximillian had replaced his usual mask with a hood like the ones Madame's fire tops wore in Paris. It covered his face and neck, down to the collar of his black t-shirt, and had a narrow mesh strip barely wide enough for his eyes. Long, protective gloves covered both forearms.

When Octavia felt better, Quinn needed to ask her about the process and what all the equipment was called, like the long metal wand with the end covered in white, cottony material, for instance. He dipped the tip into a bowl of liquid, and the cold, sharp, familiar odor of rubbing alcohol filled the air.

She tensed at what would come next when he lit the cotton.

An orange and blue flare spiked with a whoosh, then fell back, flame hugging the material at the tip of the wand like a marshmallow at a campfire.

The flickering light illuminated his arm, spotlighting a scarred area of skin by his elbow, just past the edge of the long glove. The hair was missing there—an old burn? Safety equipment on the counter reminded her of what Octavia had said about edge play, about how there was such a thin line, if it were a distinct line at all, between thrill and danger.

Maximillian brought the wand over his sub until it hovered just above her skin and moved in a slow, sweeping motion over her body. The second hand of the wall clock, the occasional movements of the fire tops, the fire's hushed hiss and crackle, the sub's breathing, Quinn's own pulse— they were the only sounds in the room as he continued his slow traverse millimeters above the woman's back.

When the wand went out, he paused long enough to dip it in the liquid and started again. Quinn imagined the feel of the radiating heat, as if she were the one on the table.

After several cycles, Maximillian nodded to the spotter on his left, and the man handed him another wand. This one reminded her of a golf club. She could picture Maximillian golfing, and she wondered what type of work he did. Each time she had seen him, his mask—and now the hood— obscured his features, but his height, his carriage, his diction led her to picture a skyscraper bustling with wealthy people. Maybe he was a stockbroker or a financier.

He soaked the wand head in the alcohol and paused, an

artist contemplating where to place his first stroke, then drew it slowly down from the woman's shoulder blades, along the back of one leg, and down to her heel in one long, smooth, deliberate line.

Goose bumps rose on Quinn's arms imagining the icy feel of the liquid and the heat to follow.

The flame shimmied down the path he laid, hungrily consuming the alcohol, and he trailed his gloved hand immediately behind it, extinguishing it. She and the spotters watched, listened. The swirling, changing colors, the hissing sound, they stretched seconds into minutes, minutes into a blur. No wonder in Paris she had lost all track of time.

Before Quinn knew it, Maximillian's motions slowed and came to a standstill, and the spotters began cleaning up before slipping quietly out of the room.

Her eyes traveled up Maximillian's arms, drawn to his hooded face. His gaze generated an intense heat all its own.

How long had he been watching her?

His submissive lifted and turned her head, resting on her other cheek. Slowly, Maximillian broke their gaze, reached behind him for a coil of black rope, and bound the woman's hands behind her back. It was okay now that the fire was safely extinguished and the spotters had removed the fuel, but it wouldn't have been a few moments ago— Octavia didn't allow bondage in the fire room.

He covered the woman with a blanket and patted her back. He tended to her dutifully, but he kept an eye on Quinn. She should leave him alone to take care of his playmate, but her legs seemed to have a different idea. He pointed with an upturned hand toward the table.

Next?

The St. Andrew's wheel demo sprung to mind, how deftly he had moved, how decisive and sure, and how quickly she had gotten lost, her legs unsteady when it was time to step down a short time later.

She shook her head no.

But truth be told, she wanted to. To float in the state this woman was in. To have the disappointment and pain, the what ifs, the regrets all melt into the heat.

The skin on her back tingled and warmed imagining she was the one on the table. But there was only one man she would trust near her body with fire, and that man was no longer hers to ask.

Maximillian held her gaze a moment longer, widened his eyes a smidge. *Change your mind?*

She mouthed a clear *no*, and only then did he take off the gloves. She caught sight of the scar again as he moved, a reminder of the potential for danger. Perhaps he had been reckless once, although he had followed Octavia's rules to the letter tonight. Still, his scar left Quinn wondering, who was this man and what had happened in his past?

She summoned her resolve and channeled it to her feet, keeping her eyes on the door as she strode past him and out of the room.

ALEX WAS busy with a small group in the alcove outfitted like a doctor's exam room when Quinn returned to the main floor, so she made a circuit around the space to make sure everything was okay. Careful not to get close enough to interrupt a scene, she watched the tops for signs of distraction or overzealousness and, from the bottoms, listened for safe words or sounds of unintended distress. It could be hard to discern cries of pleasure from pain, so she watched each scene for a moment and went with her gut instinct, just as Octavia had instructed before the 101 class and as Quinn had done when she interrupted Madame in Paris.

On her second slow lap around the floor, Alex waved to catch her eye and jogged toward her. His chest rose and fell rapidly once he stopped. "We have a fluids issue. Blood. And someone needs to walk the floor on level three—I haven't gone up there in a while. You have a preference?"

"I'll go up." The sight of blood sometimes made her woozy. So much for big-girl undies.

"You sure?" He eyed her skeptically. By now, all the DMs and many of the members knew she felt more comfortable with the clothing-not-optional policy down here.

"I got this." She made a fist and shook it for effect.

Letting out a relieved breath, he met her hand in a fist bump. "That's the spirit."

He ran back in the direction he had come from, and she unhooked the braided burgundy velvet rope strung across the staircase. The metal clanked faintly as she re-hooked it, the sound fading into the music coming from the speaker overhead.

Upstairs, black-and-white images of fetish balls at what she recognized as the manor lined the wall—artistic, sensual scenes with faces turned away or obscured by masks and feathery plumes.

Quinn paused briefly at the closed doors of each private room, listening for trouble. She didn't want to eavesdrop, but she also didn't want to miss a sign that someone might need help.

At the end of the hall, she paused at the archway to the open central area. It looked like an old-fashioned Paris hotel lobby might look, with round burgundy couches in the middle, their cylindrical backs button-tufted, and alcoves filled with velvet sectionals. Tall, lush potted plants partitioned and softened the space, giving some—but not much—shielding to the scenes unfolding in each nook. She tried not to look in the direction of the sounds—a switch hitting flesh, cries of pleasure, skin spanking skin—although she wanted to. There was so much about the lifestyle she wanted to learn but, absent a sound of distress, she would not peep through the leaves; she was not a voyeur.

But when a muffled moan caught her attention, instinctively she turned toward the noise.

It was the woman from the fire room, Maximillian's sub. She was seated low in a chair, her arms bound around the back, a harness of intricate knots descending her torso. Her ankles were bound to the legs of the chair, her knees pulled apart and tied where the arms of the chair met the seat. Except for the vertical line of the knots, she was naked and open to him, completely exposed. A ball gag filled her mouth, explaining the stifled sound.

Quinn looked from the woman to Maximillian, without his fire hood but masked once again. His chest was bare now, his tight black pants a second skin, uniform and smooth, except for the prominent rise that stretched the material taut between his hips.

And now Quinn saw why the woman moaned. Not only was she rocking against a strategically placed knot, but he had attached clamps to both her nipples and with quick, rhythmic dips of his index finger, he tugged the thin metal chain that hung between them. With his next tug, another moan drifted from the woman's mouth.

As if his eyes followed the sound to Quinn's ears, his gaze locked onto hers.

Aha, you've entered my lair.

Of course he would mistake her attention, her inability

to drag her eyes away from their scene, for the desire to be in his submissive's place. And maybe it was desire, but not for or with him.

Embarrassed, she turned away. She was here to work, not think about Jonathan. Or his reunion with Delphine.

After walking the hallway once more and finding nothing worrying up here, she hurried down the stairs to the main floor, unhooked the velvet rope, and re-clipped it behind her.

At closing time, she helped Alex take out the trash and texted Octavia to see if she needed anything before Quinn caught the train home. The three dots appeared and stopped, appeared and stopped, and . . .

Maximillian's voice startled her. "It's been quite an eventful evening for you—first the fireroom and then the upper play area. What did you think of Octavia's den of iniquity on level three? I take it your foray was intriguing?"

Uppaah. She really wondered about that accent, and she pictured his mocking smile from the way the mask crinkled by the corner of the thin mouth slit. He was making fun of how she separated BDSM play and sex. At least at the club. He didn't know her or what she did outside Octavia's with Jonathan—what she *had done* with Jonathan, past tense.

She looked at him without answering. It was disconcerting not to see his face, not to hear his real manner of speaking, not to have some idea of how old he was. From his voice, she guessed early forties, but just about everything about him was impossible to know. Even his eyes were unreadable, and weren't they supposed to be windows to the soul?

In perfecting his club persona, he had erased the real man.

Before Paris, she couldn't have imagined keeping such a secret, going to such great lengths—the mask, the accent, the whole air of mystery—to hide who you were. But then yesterday Leigh had asked why she had been so quiet the past several days and, rather than explain her trip to Paris, Quinn's heartbeat had pounded in her chest as she flat-out lied.

"Do consider my offer from last time," Maximillian said. "There's a great deal of knowledge I could impart to you, since you're so eager to learn."

13

PROSE

Quinn closed the notebook and set the pen on her writing desk. Cool evening air drifted into her study through the window she had cracked open when she sat down two—or was it three?—hours ago. Her hand ached, a wonderfully satisfied and familiar tiredness. It wasn't the best prose she had ever written, nor was there a lot of it, but after such a long absence, she had written.

After more than a year, new words graced the pages, her mind freed of excess clutter. Maybe it was Paris, the time at Madame's, that inspired her subconscious, gave her the start of a short, fictional story. Or maybe it was time itself. Or some combination. Whatever the catalyst, a barely perceptible force had drawn her to her desk, drawn her to one of the new Paris notebooks, to her favorite pen, to the familiar seat of her chair, and she had written.

Sadness still circled, but there was newfound peace in it. She missed Harris with every cell in her body. Some days, some moments, were especially brutal, grief tightening its hold and squeezing as if it never would let go. She would miss him forever. But a long, happy marriage was an incredible gift—many people didn't get to experience that once in a lifetime. It was naive, perhaps greedy, to think she might receive such a gift twice. Falling for Jonathan had been a mistake.

She had been stupid to indulge her inner voice in Paris, the voice that longed for him, the voice that caused a flicker of hope for a future with him, the voice she had planned to use to call him when she got back to New York.

Until she saw the tabloids at the airport.

His reconciliation with Delphine might sting right now. It might make Quinn's chest ache all over again. But it was for the best.

Definitely for the best.

She pictured him tonight at the gala awards ceremony Leigh mentioned he would be attending. Dapper and accomplished and uber-sexy in his tuxedo, with Delphine— no doubt even more glamorous and charming than she appeared in photographs—standing beside him. Where, with their bond, their history, she belonged.

Good for him. Quinn wanted him to be happy.

But this was all the thinking about him, and him together with Delphine, she would allow herself tonight. The wisp of smoke in the air from a neighbor's woodstove reminded her that earlier this afternoon she had planned to get the firepit ready for Becca's reception—pull the dried, overgrown grass, add more stones to shore up the wall, replace the rotting tree-stump seats that encircled it with fresh logs Jerome had kindly left. Instead of working outside, though, she had gone to her desk. She would write again tomorrow, she was sure of it. But now it was time to refocus on the wedding and, tonight's project, the firepit.

To have a fireside afterglow was Becca's idea. "Charles

loves campfires," she had said excitedly a couple of weeks ago, when she, Leigh, and Quinn had passed the firepit on their way to the barn to give the caterer a tour. "It'll be the perfect way for us to kick back with our friends after the reception."

It was a great idea, Quinn agreed, made all the better by how enthusiastic Becca had been to do it for him.

Quinn had a good feeling about the two of them, an intuition they would last.

She threw on a sweater, found her gardening gloves in the basket by the back door, and went outside to get started.

Item number one: At the chest-high woodpile beside the barn, she adjusted and tightened the tarp to better keep out the moisture. There would be no campfire with soggy wood. Since the wedding was still a week away, she made a silent pact with the universe: Rain all week if you must, but please, please, please, not next Saturday; don't let anything spoil Becca and Charles's special day.

14

MARIONETTE

J onathan coughed, sending a puff of powder into the air. It was hard to think of a place he hated more than the makeup chair. It had nothing to do with Lizzie, who was a fine makeup artist as far as he could tell, or that he deemed himself too macho. No. What bugged him was the fakeness, how the crap on his face was like wearing a mask, how it made him look like Geppetto carved him from wood.

"Once more—hold your breath, close your eyes." Lizzie held her brush steady, just off his nose, waiting to apply more. At least it was only a couple of times a year. No one insisted on makeup when he shot on location, at least not yet. It was probably only a matter of time before Clay suggested it. If his face got shiny with oil and sweat, he used a towel or a bandanna or a couple of squares of toilet paper to wipe away the sheen. Good to go.

"Ready?" Lizzie asked.

How did women stand this? He braced himself. "Ready." The brush swept against the other side of his nose, under his eye, across his forehead.

"Make him extra pretty." Mike came to stand behind him, and he patted Jonathan's shoulder through the cape Lizzie had draped over him. "Big night, J.J. When you're done here, we have our slot scheduled with the stage manager for the run-through. Can you send me your speech?" He nodded at Jonathan's phone on the counter in front of him. "I'll make sure it's loaded into the teleprompter."

"Yeah, sure. It's the generic thank yous to the team . . . If you clue me in on what we're up for, I can fill in the missing bits." He tapped out an email to Mike on his phone and attached the file.

"Meet me on stage when you're done here—we'll go through it together."

When Lizzie cut him loose, he found Mike onstage in the event space, a concert hall on steroids that spanned several floors of the company's flagship building. The teams from the network's other travel shows sat in clusters among the otherwise empty theater seats. Seats that in a couple of hours would fill with industry players: competing networks attending under the guise of camaraderie that really were scouting talent, advertisers awaiting the pucker of Mike's and Maddie's—and the other execs'—lips on their asses, reporters and bloggers and social media influencers that made him feel old.

The awards might be a big deal among cable travel networks, but they were not exactly the Emmys.

The stage manager positioned him at the podium, a tilted slab of clear acrylic attached to a thin metal stand that matched the auditorium's modern, minimalistic style. He took the index cards from his tux pocket and put them on the leather blotter in front of him, then put on his reading glasses.

Mike and Clay didn't like him using the cards, but he insisted on having them as a backup. Teleprompters could crap out, and it was hard not to stumble when your lines suddenly vanished before your eyes.

That would suck, especially tonight. With Mike having been so tight-lipped, maybe *Spice of Life* really was about to win a Compass. Best Show? Best Host? Best Directing? He didn't want anything to go awry.

Speaking of fuck-ups, he checked his fly and shimmied the ends of his bowtie so it sat straight, brushed his index finger past his nostrils to check for wayward nose hair, and ran his tongue along the front of his teeth even though he had avoided the spinach quiche at the luncheon.

High-def TV could be a bastard.

For once, for a second, he let himself consider the possibility of winning as real and warranted, not just another lucky break. It might have been the successful travel expo events in Paris and the time with Delphine—he finally felt he was regaining his stride. He stifled the old voices, those little fuckers perched on his shoulder who hissed, *Luck runs out.*

He checked his index cards again to make sure they were in the right order and glanced up at the teleprompter to confirm it was displaying his speech. That snafu happened too often—a presenter starting to deliver someone else's words until that awkward, public realization. He was used to going off script—he did it all the time during shooting, at least he used to—but to a live audience, everyone armed with a smartphone? That was way too risky.

The first few words matched, the ones where he said the name of his show and that he was honored to be here tonight.

So far, so good.

The stage manager moved to face him across the podium. "When you first come out, sweep your eyes over the audience, left to right, one-Mississippi, two-Mississippi, three-Mississippi, and don't forget the mezzanine—I put a cue in the prompter and added you saying, 'Wow, what a crowd. What a night,' and you'll nod a hint when you say it. Okay?"

"Got it."

"You'll start the speech, and we've marked the spots in the text where you'll pause for the audience to laugh." She gestured behind her when she referred to the audience, then turned back toward him.

"Okay, yep, got it." *Not my first rodeo*. In its earliest years, the show had been nominated three times for a Compass.

Turn. Laugh. Gesture. Might as well remind him not to sweat or pick his nose or adjust his sac. The detailed direction wasn't unreasonable, but sheesh, why not just attach strings to his wrists so they could move him how they wanted, a fucking marionette.

All the styling and handholding was another reminder of how this gig had changed. When he interviewed people on his show, he encouraged them to be themselves. He might remind them to look at the camera now and then, but the whole point was to show the audience who they were.

"And when Clay comes out, you'll side-step over about this much—" she held up her hands to show the distance— "so you're both centered behind the lectern."

Mike raised his finger to interrupt and stepped closer. "Great news, J.J.—*Spice of Life* is winning a Compass for Best Showrunner!" He extended his hand to shake Jonathan's. "I made a coupla tweaks to your speech to recognize Clay for all he's done, including coming up with version 2.0 and the new direction."

Mike dropped Jonathan's hand and looked at the stage manager. "Let's advance the script so we can rehearse the edited lines before Clay gets here. He doesn't know yet; I want him to be surprised."

What. The. Fuck.

His mind blanked as he tried to process the information dump Mike had just taken. That Clay was winning the Compass, that apparently the f'ed up new direction was a done deal, that Mike, who was a jerk on his best day, gave a rat's ass about protecting Clay's surprise.

His fists clenched as his mind cycled from confusion to white hot anger. But he should stay calm, choose his battles wisely. After all, he did have his own travel show—sort of.

He cleared his throat. "New direction?"

"Yeah, the one we talked about the other day, you know, bringing in your wife. We called, ran the idea by her. She's interested in having a conversation. But right now, you need to run your lines. We only have a minute."

The stage manager stepped aside so he could read the new crap Mike added. This ought to be good. *Wait.* "You *talked* to Delphine?"

"Unless you have another wife—"

"*Ex*-wife."

"Whatever. She's interested. Rumor has it the winery is struggling since daddy died; my guess is she could use the money. Right now, keep your panties from twisting and let's read your lines."

He read Mike's lines. His voice sounded wooden and hollow while his mind raced.

Not only a marionette, but a ventriloquist's dummy, too.

"Um, Mr. Jaines, let's try again, this time with more passion." The stage manager looked at Mike, concerned.

"That's all the passion I got." He turned to Mike. "We'll have to talk about this on Monday."

Mike stepped closer and took hold of Jonathan's forearm just below his elbow. "Look, here it is, J.J.: Clay and I plotted out where *Spice of Life* is going. We ran some quick focus groups, and it was just as we expected—the advertisers are all over the idea. So, happy to loop you in going forward, but the decision is not up for discussion."

The stage manager's face tightened with worry and she was breaking out in a not-so-fine sheen of sweat. "Don't worry," Jonathan told her, "I'll give it what I got." He picked up his cards and left the stage.

Air. He needed air. He snuck out the hall's backstage door to the alley, which had the added benefit of avoiding the mingling and ass-kissing that would be happening in the lobby as the audience arrived and eventually filed into the auditorium.

He checked the time now and then and, when he couldn't put it off any longer, hurried back inside and slipped into his seat with minimal interaction. Dutiful, ready to put on a smiling face. Ready to say a bunch of shit he didn't mean, stuffing his feelings to avoid rocking the boat, acting like he agreed with a change that would send his show to the shitter and do who-knows-what to Delphine.

The lights dimmed. Maddie kicked off the ceremony, her scripted remarks eliciting bursts of collective laughter on cue, and he stewed.

Already, he knew what Mike would say next time they talked: It's a great opportunity; if you don't want to host *this* show, J.J., someone else will. It was the same shit Jonathan had been saying to himself over the years, as the network had gutted what *Spice of Life* once was.

Most of the changes to the show hadn't sat right with him. But he had kept quiet, told himself they were small, no big deal.

One by one, taking his best hole-in-the-wall finds off the shooting schedules, getting cozy with large hotel chains, and, yeah, that ridiculous private jet cabin scene filmed in a mock setup at a hangar in Jersey. If that hadn't shown him the writing on the wall, what would?

He had become a master at crediting luck for his success, not daring to say or do anything that might jeopardize it. Along the way, he had silenced his good instincts and let people down—namely himself.

But he knew.

This shitty show idea that would tie Delphine and him to each other in ways that weren't healthy for either of them?

Wrong.

A job with a network that had brought a showrunner in over his head to take charge of *his* show, the show he built on his old tour business, his relationships, his way of seeing things, and mutate it into travel porn for the rich and famous?

Wrong.

Mike often tried to smooth the mismatch between Jonathan's and Clay's ideas by saying there was an audience for that kind of show. Of course there was. It just wasn't his.

Funny how you could blame others for doing a number on you when, in reality, you could take most of the credit yourself. By swallowing their crap, by not pushing back because he feared what he might lose rather than what he might gain—a new and different audience, pride in his work, self-respect—he had done their work for them, transformed the show into something neither it nor he was.

Mike and Clay hadn't been his worst enemies, Jonathan had been his own.

He looked at his watch. The stage manager ran a tight ship, so the time slot she had given him for presenting would be accurate, and it was still an hour and a half away.

Why the ever-loving fuck was he sitting here?

HUNCHED, with a hand on his seat to keep it from snapping up, he stood and whispered *excuse me, pardon me* as he squeezed past each pair of knees.

Mike sat two rows up, three seats in from the aisle. Jonathan went to the end of his row, crouched, and reached over the people in the first two seats to tap his arm. "I'm leaving," he said. He was done with whispering. He pointed toward the theater doors behind them.

Mike did a double-take, looking at him, the stage, and back at him, confusion clouding his eyes. "But you go on in . . ."

"Leaving. For good."

He didn't wait for Mike's response. Work wasn't the only area of his life that he was going to change, effective immediately.

Quinn was another perfect example of how he took what was offered. Early on, he had wound himself tight waiting, time after time, for her to text, to beckon him, not daring to ask her for another meeting. Not daring to break their silence, not daring to show her the affection he felt.

The radio silence that stretched between them now was because she was afraid. He got that, and that's why—he told himself—he had not shared his feelings with her. Those feelings were largely why it bothered him so much she belonged to the club, and opening up to her might have helped her understand where he was coming from. Might have helped her realize he wasn't the jealous lover trying to cage her. Or that he wasn't the guy playing knight in shining armor on a mission to protect her. He did feel protective of her certainly, but he knew perfectly well she didn't need him to be—she was so strong, more than capable of protecting herself.

His feelings about the club extended way beyond that. It was about the two of them as a couple, with—he hoped like hell—a shared future. But how could she know? He hadn't told her. *I'm in love with you. I want more.*

I want more.

Nope. Hadn't said it. He had been telling himself she wasn't ready to hear it, and maybe that was true. But maybe it also was an excuse, so he could avoid the possibility of rejection. To avoid losing the good and undeserved fortune that had dropped into his lap that night she sent Gil away with his car.

You lucky son of a bitch; don't fuck it up.

That had been his exact thought since the beginning with her. Story of his life. Jesus, a shrink would have a field day. It was the same approach he had taken to the show and to his marriage—*you have so much; don't dare to want more.*

But he was wasting skills, talent, love. Ignoring those gifts was giving the middle finger to the universe, and that was not a great life strategy.

As he hurried out of the auditorium to the lobby, he took his phone from his inner jacket pocket. Pausing against a pillar, he opened the transit authority app, scanned the schedule, and selected the next train north.

Friday night. She might not be home. She might be at the club.

Might, might, might.

He looked at the dark gray capital letters on his wrist —*DARE*—and shook his head at the guy who had, during a dark time, needed that tattoo. He knew in his gut that certain things you had to walk away from, no matter what you might lose. And other things you had to move toward, no matter what you might risk. Had he really needed the indelible reminder etched into his skin to live his life that way?

He hit "purchase" in the app and, as his train ticket appeared on the screen, he headed for the door.

"Hey, man, where're you going?" It was Book, short for Booker, a chopper pilot for the network's weather channels, coming out of the men's room.

"Grand Central. Going to see a friend."

"Where's your friend?"

"Up in the Hudson Valley."

"Can I give you a lift? I need to bring the bird to the hangar across the river. And the longer I'm out, the less I have to sit through." He motioned toward the auditorium.

"That'd be fantastic."

"Meet you at the helipad in five. Gotta grab my flight bag from my office." Book headed left and Jonathan went right, toward the staff elevator, which gave a slight jounce when it reached the top floor. The doors slid open, and lights flicked on in the long hallway as Jonathan headed to the industrial door to the roof. He pulled it open, and a flash of panic gripped him hard when that heavy metal panel slammed shut behind him.

No turning back. Mike probably cut off his access already anyway.

The night was clear and cool and dry, an energizing contrast to the musty smell in the hallway. The helicopter was tied down over a large yellow H painted on the cement a few yards away. He walked toward it, then past it to stand at the guardrail to look out. The sudden sense of calm confirmed that quitting was the right, and not reckless, thing to do. Same sense he had gotten right after he had told his parents he was dropping out of college twenty-something years ago to take a shitty job abroad.

While he waited for Book, he took off his heavy diving watch, a "gift" from an advertiser that expected it to be worn in public and—oh, so subtle—photographed in an agreed-upon percentage of images in his social media feeds. He put it in his pocket. On Monday, he gladly would return it to Mike.

There would be other issues to work out, too, like his contract for starters. But he had decided to walk. That was progress.

The metal door slammed again and when he turned, Book was jogging toward the copter. He set his bag on the cement and began his pre-flight check.

Once they were tucked into the cockpit, Book finished his preparations and handed Jonathan a green headset. The blades whirred and Book gave him a thumbs up. A few seconds later, the skids left the ground and air buoyed the body, upward drift.

They rose into the sky and turned, the city shrouded in darkness but glittering, one hundred eighty degrees around them.

Book followed the Hudson River, inky and not so sharply defined at this time of night, not unlike Jonathan's plans for the future.

In Paris, he and Delphine had finally put their relationship behind them. For the first time since she had slapped his face and ripped the painting a couple of years ago, he could stop obsessively peering in that rearview mirror and instead look out the windshield at what he wanted to do with the rest of his life.

As for his next career move, he could knock on the network's competitors' doors, likely get a similar job hosting a similar show. That Explore had brought Clay in as showrunner—a move that didn't go unnoticed by the industry—made it less likely Jonathan would land that executive role. But even if he did, he still would be a marionette. It would just be another Mike, another Maddie, a fresh set of advertisers pulling the strings.

The business idea he had tucked away since forever elbowed its way forward. He could revisit it, seriously look at what it would take to make it reality. He had built a successful company once—small, granted—and it had led him to *Spice of Life*. This idea was a whole other level, but he knew the industry, knew the good people to involve, and the assholes to avoid. He didn't have the kind of money required to fund it himself, but he could find investors who would share his vision.

Why the fuck not?

"Man, it is one great night for flying." Book's intensity softened into pure pleasure as he pointed out the familiar landmarks—Central Park, Columbia University, the George Washington Bridge, Yankee Stadium, the Palisades. All places Jonathan knew well from the ground. They looked so different from up here.

It's called perspective, dumbass. Maybe he was finally gaining some.

As he looked out the bug-eye window, he noticed the trash bag hanging from a low hook on the door. He reached into his pocket, pulled out his Explore Network badge, and dropped it in. Book's brow and eyes squinched. "Hold up, that's for trash. Give it to me, I'll leave it in your office."

"It *is* trash."

"But isn't that your . . ."

"Yep." Getting rid of his security badge solved nothing. He would pay a price for up and walking out, tonight of all nights. But right now, however symbolic, it felt right.

Book laughed. "Good for you. Hey, I heard one of the weather shows needs a host. I can put in a good word . . ."

"Thanks, that's okay. I'm actually thinking about doing something on my own. I've had this crazy idea for a while."

Book looked at him, dead serious. "Well, then do it, man. Why not? We only go around once. Let me know if I can help. Crazy ideas are my specialty."

"I'll be in touch. Buy you a beer or three. Also, I might need an expert pilot."

"I can find you one of those." He flashed a big smile. "Hey man, for what it's worth, I used to love your show."

Used to. That tidily summed up why Jonathan had just left the network and his show. He used to love it too.

Onward.

Out the chopper windshield, the river continued to unspool, one long, black ribbon that reminded him of Quinn's silken scarf. The rest of this night would be all about her, assuming she was home and would hear him out.

Like his immediate career prospects, she was anything but safe. Hell no, she was a blindfolded cliff-dive into an ocean of risk and potential heartbreak. And more than anything, he needed to see her.

15

TERRIBLE LIAR

Quinn stepped back and assessed the firepit. Moths and mosquitoes flew into the light from the flood lamp at the corner of the barn roof. The job had taken a few hours, but it was time well spent. She had pulled the feathery, over-grown grass and moved it to the compost pile. Fit the river stones back together into a low wall. Made a cozy ring of tree stumps for Becca and Charles and their closest friends to sit around the fire.

As she pictured the scene, she cataloged the sounds that filled the air: a katydid's chirp and rattle, waves lapping the neighbor's dock, the bleat of a helicopter rotor, voices floating up from a sailboat on the river. Next weekend, laughter and music would join the nighttime chorus.

The thought she had kept at bay as she hauled rocks and tugged out tufts of grass began to creep back in: Jonathan would come to the wedding, and now that he was back together with Delphine, she would come with him. Which meant Quinn would have to watch the two of them together.

Dancing. Laughing. Holding hands. Kissing.

She thought of Madame's homemade salve, wondered if it could ease the sting of salt rubbed into a wound like this.

A half-moon lit the sky as she went into the barn to shut off the floodlight and noticed a honeycomb ball wedged beneath the soffit. She would call the exterminator first thing Monday morning. It might be wasps, and she did not want anyone at the wedding to unwittingly stir up the nest.

She grabbed a wool blanket from the shelf underneath the workbench, turned off the light switch, and pulled the large doors along the metal track until they were closed. It was such a beautiful night, too nice to go inside yet.

On the deck overlooking the river, she dropped the blanket on one of the teak Adirondack chairs and leaned against the railing. The chairs had sat on the porch of the old house, facing out to the water. Harris had insisted on having them made from teak, for its longevity, he had said.

Back then, she could not have imagined the events that would lead her here, without him, the sharp corners she could not possibly have seen around.

But she would not have done anything differently had she known what would happen—she would not have traded her time with Harris for anything—not any amount of money, not another man, not avoidance of the sorrow of losing him.

She had been telling herself she was scared of a relationship with Jonathan, that she wasn't ready. Would there ever be a fixed point in time, an official date, when she would feel ready to take a chance like she and Harris had, like Becca and Charles would next weekend? A distinct moment when every what-if vanished? Just as she would always grieve for Harris, she would probably always feel lingering fear about letting herself love someone new.

She recalled the icebreaker exercise the Hollinger fellows at the artists colony played after dinner on the first night. Someone called out a word, and the participants had to write the first antonym that came to mind. It had been fascinating to hear the surprising range of opposites people came up with. You started the game thinking in black and white, certain there was only one logical word to complete each pair, but you ended up seeing entirely new possibilities.

Love, risk.

She had kept herself busy the past few weeks planning the wedding, helping at the club, taking that unexpected trip to Paris with Octavia to experience something completely unfamiliar, and none of it had erased the truth. She missed Jonathan. She cared for him. She trusted him. She wouldn't do anything to get in the way of his happiness with Delphine, but she needed to set things right. She needed to talk to him, to say some last things.

Thank you for taking such good care of me. I'm sorry I wasn't ready to take a chance.

It was a conversation for the two of them, not three, and she didn't want to have it at Becca's reception. Better to clear the air between them now, so it wouldn't be awkward next weekend. She picked up her phone from where she had left it on the wide arm of the chair, wrapped the blanket around herself, and started a fresh text.

Hi. Can we talk?

Delete. Delete. Delete. It sounded desperate, and he would assume she wanted more than just to talk. And then, to quell any expectations on her part, he would preface his response by telling her about Delphine. *Sure, we can talk, but there's something you should know . . .*

Quinn already knew all she needed to about their reconciliation.

Another helicopter rose higher in the sky, while distant peals of laughter and a deep bass beat came from a party boat, lights strung between the masts. A minute later, a train whistle broke the darkness with one long sound, a signal to the station in town. Since moving here, she had begun to learn the language. This horn differed from the wailing dirge of the freight trains, the mournful cry that had set off her nightmare the first night here with Jonathan.

The night she kissed him.

Moving to a new house, the underscore of that sorrowful sound, that kiss. The trio had unfurled a tsunami of emotions, and she was not prepared to be overtaken by the feelings that emerged from her nightmare. Jonathan had tried to comfort her so sweetly, to be the antidote to the threat. But that was impossible because he was both.

Love, risk.

It was too late for them now, but if she were open to it, maybe she could let herself fall in love again someday.

She started the text over.

Hey. Meet for a cup of coffee sometime soon?

BOOK DROPPED him off in an empty parking lot down the hill from Quinn's, well away from her property so a chopper landing in her yard wouldn't frighten her.

If she was home.

He jogged up the long street toward the break in the

fieldstone wall that ran around her place, slowed to catch his breath, then re-tucked his shirt and smoothed his cummerbund. This visit was important.

He strode across the field. The house was dark; so was the barn. Shit, maybe she really wasn't home. But then his eyes found her on the deck. She stood at the railing looking out over the river, a blanket wrapped around her like a long cape.

Even in the darkness, even with her covered up, he could feel her nearby. He would recognize her body anywhere. Seeing her silhouette made his stomach drop, like when a plane hits an air pocket, weightless and compressed at the same time.

His phone vibrated, and he took it out of his jacket pocket. She was far enough away still that she wouldn't hear his rustling. He stifled a laugh when he saw the waiting text message—it was from her.

Hey. Meet for a cup of coffee sometime soon?

He tapped out his response, grinning like a fool at the perfect opening she handed him.

Sure. Love to.

. . .

Great. When's a good time?

He kept his eyes on her as he walked swiftly toward the deck. Her head was down; she was focused on her screen.

No time like the present, sweetheart.

The night was quiet and he didn't want to startle her, so

he modulated his voice as he got close. "Milk, no sugar, if I recall."

She whipped around, clapping a hand to her chest. So much for not startling her. Her eyes went wide as he joined her on the deck. "What are you doing here?"

"I needed to see you."

Her carriage, her expression, they registered surprise, then fleeting relief, and something else he couldn't read. Sadness? Wistfulness? Regret? He wasn't sure, but as she faced him, she reminded him of a wide-eyed doe caught in fast-moving headlights.

"Hey," he said, taking a step closer so he could take her arms in his hands. He didn't like how she looked at him.

Her thick blanket was scratchy, the kind you kept in the trunk in case your car got stuck in a snowstorm. "It's me, Quinn. Come here." He wanted her against him. They were mere inches apart but not close enough; he wanted more.

She hesitated, but then moved closer and leaned against him. The sigh she let out as their bodies came together and he wrapped his arms around her made his soul ache. He had missed her so fucking much.

"I'm here." She looked up into his eyes, her head tipped slightly. Her shoulders drooped as she sighed again, as if the sight of him broke her heart.

"What's wrong?" he asked. The charged air between them made the idea of meeting for coffee absurd. "You first —what did you want to talk about?"

HIS VOICE WAS LOW, almost hoarse. Its roughness made her dizzy. Now that he was standing in front of her, she wouldn't be able to take another minute like this—against him, his breath in her hair, inhaling his scent as he held her when he belonged to someone else.

But there was demand in his voice, need. *It's me, Quinn. Come here.*

It was barely a step, more an effortless moving into him. This was what he was asking for, she could tell by the ease in how their bodies moved together, the way he enveloped her in his arms.

Heat emanated from him—his thighs, his torso, his hands. She leaned against his chest, his bowtie brushing the top of her head.

With her hand on his chest, she leaned back and met his gaze. "I wanted to say I'm sorry."

"You don't have to apologize." He brought his forehead to touch hers.

"I do. I need to explain," she said, moving back, trying to reach for the right words, like grasping at strings of floating balloons to tug them down and say them. "I couldn't keep doing what we were doing. I wasn't ready to face the feelings I have—had," she corrected, "for you, but I shouldn't have pushed you away so harshly, so abruptly. You deserved better than that. And I wanted to say thank you. For everything you gave me."

He tried to pull her in, but she pushed back on his chest. She wasn't done. Any closer and she would lose her grip on the few balloons she managed to hold. "And I wanted to say I hope it works out. I'm happy for you, and I wish you two the best."

Her voice cracked, nearly breaking the last sentence in two.

His eyes narrowed at first, like he was confused, and then his lips inched into a knowing, teasing smile.

"Don't laugh, it's not funny." He would leave soon, and that would be that. She bit her quivering lip to fend off the waiting tears.

"You're happy for me that I'm . . . back with Delphine?"

She sniffled and nodded.

"How happy?" With his thumb, he wiped the droplet trickling down her cheek. He continued the caress until he had traced her cheekbone, and now both his hands were holding her face. "Because you don't seem very happy." His eyes smiled as he spoke, his laugh lines wrinkled.

"I am. Happy."

He laughed from way down deep, and it resounded in her chest. "You have a wonderful imagination for fiction, Quinn Layborn, but you're a *terrible* liar."

"You're a good man; you deserve a second chance, and you have one now. So I am . . ." With her eyes square on his chest, she nodded vigorously and smoothed his lapel. ". . . truly happy for you."

His smile went full wattage. "You shouldn't look at gossip rags or believe what you read online. You know better."

It took her a moment to process. "Are you saying it's not true? You're not back together?"

"We're not back together."

She expelled the breath she had not been aware of holding, relief filling her every pore. "Well, in that case, I am a little happy." She brought her thumb and index fingers together, *a teensy bit,* and put her arms around him. "But then what happened in Paris?"

"Delphine surprised me at the travel expo. We had dinner. It was good to reconnect on different terms, and it was the most straightforward we ever were with each other. She spent the night in my room—"

Quinn coughed, an involuntary sputter. "I see."

"I slept on the couch, Quinn. Somewhere between midnight and sunrise, it finally sunk in after way too long. The story I had been telling myself about how much I fucked up that marriage wasn't the full truth. I mean, yes, me fucking up was true—I was unfaithful, no excuses.

"But our marriage wasn't an enchanted fairy tale I sabotaged. I fucked up by marrying someone I wasn't in love with. I married the safe choice. Because I didn't dare believe I deserved, or would find, more."

"But the photos I saw, they were so intimate. It looked like you kissed—or more."

"We were married, we were close once—it's easy for that to come through in pictures. But we didn't kiss. We didn't have sex. She asked, but I said no. If you think I could make love to another woman, you don't realize the effect you've had on me."

He brought his hand to the back of her neck and massaged her skin, while she pressed against him, wrapped him in the blanket with her, felt him getting hard.

"Yes, that kind of effect also," he joked.

They laughed together as his hands found her hips, just the way they used to, and she reached for his face, brought hers close to meet it. Their mouths touched softly at first, then parted so they could taste each other again.

"I've missed you so much," she whispered, his agreement dusting her lips like sugar.

She stroked the skin on the back of his neck, brushed her fingers over his short hair, touched his face, his throat, his shoulders, his chest. There was so much of him to learn. That prospect made her shiver and, without moving her mouth from his, she slipped her hands under his jacket to warm them with his heat. "Let's go inside."

16

SUNDAY MORNING? SUNDAY MORNING

She turned off the light in the kitchen and they climbed the stairs hand in hand, the wood floor creaking as they walked down the hall to her bedroom. With their phones both sitting on her dresser, his work bag leaning against it, he stepped behind her, placed his hands on her shoulders and, soon, his lips on her neck, tiny light kisses. His words teased like feathers tickling her skin. "I want to undress you."

"Please," she said, raising her arms so he could lift off her sweater and the t-shirt she wore beneath it. With a kiss to her shoulder, bare except for the strap of her bra, he reached around to unfasten her jeans.

He made quick work of them, but not so quick that he didn't pause to sweep his hand across her belly, a tender stroke. When the jeans were near the floor, she stepped out of them while he held onto her hips, his breathing uneven. His hands moved up and down along her sides, making her tremble.

"I love how your body responds to me," he said.

She crossed her arms near her waist to take hold of his hands. "I love how you touch me."

Their eyes met in the mirror as he wrapped his arms further around her, pulled her closer. "You're beautiful. You didn't let me tell you the first time we were together, but you are."

"I couldn't hear it, not from you."

"I understood." He bent his head and lightly kissed her shoulder again, letting his lips linger.

When he straightened, she sought his gaze in their reflection before turning to face him so she could get rid of the bowtie and unbutton his shirt.

"Thank you," she said, but his attention had shifted, his eyes focused over her shoulder.

"The sketch in the corner of your mirror, where did you get it?"

She had not expected this conversation, to talk about her trip to Paris, and certainly not tonight. All she had thought of was expressing her regret, wishing him well, putting her hope to rest.

Closure, indeed.

She steeled herself. When Leigh asked what she had been up to last weekend, she hadn't wanted to lie. But she also recalled how, when Leigh confronted her about the rumor she had been spotted at Octavia's all those weeks ago, there was judgment.

In Leigh's worldview, there were the *kind of people* who went to dungeons, and the kind of people who did not. She and Quinn, in that worldview, did not.

So Quinn had lied, saying an old friend invited her on a spur-of-the-moment luxury shopping trip to Paris. She didn't have any friends who would jet off to Paris for a luxury shopping weekend, but it was the first thing that popped into her head that would neatly satisfy Leigh's curiosity and not invite a volley of follow-up questions.

Leigh never would understand Quinn's need for the club, or her growing friendship with Octavia, or why she would travel to France, or anywhere for that matter, to learn from a world-renowned dominatrix.

But Quinn would not lie to Jonathan, and she braced for his reaction. "Paris, to—"

"When were you in Paris?" he interrupted.

"Would you believe last week?"

He craned his neck to see the sketch better. "I believe everything you tell me. Ah, that's why you assumed, about Delphine. I wondered, since it didn't get quite as much attention here."

"I was at the airport on my way home. I planned to call you when I landed in New York, but then I saw the papers."

He let go of her fast, hurried to his work bag, and slid a manila folder out of a large envelope. "I have to show you something."

In her bra and panties without him against her, the air was chilly, and she hugged herself while he carefully pulled a piece of white paper from the folder.

It was a sketch—Jonathan looking through a window, the same pattern of shading in the shadows, the marker lines the same thickness and drawing style as hers.

She took her sketch from the mirror frame, closed her eyes, and assessed the weight and texture of both sheets at the same time.

The two leaves felt identical.

She thought back to the busker who approached her as she left the stationery shop. And how, while deciding on notebooks, she had gotten such a strong sense of Jonathan in that moment.

That wasn't really possible, was it, that he had actually been right there? "Where were you when he drew it?"

"On a cobblestone street in the eighteenth, across from a park, outside a bookstore . . . no, a paper shop."

"Last weekend—Sunday morning?"

"Sunday morning," he said.

She went to her nightstand, picked up the notebook she now kept there, and raised it to show him. "Cute little shop with a metal sculpture of a fountain pen hanging over the door?"

He nodded.

"I bought a bunch of these there last Sunday morning. I was thinking about you while I was inside—it was like I *felt* you there—and when I came out, he drew that. That's what he saw in my expression, in my eyes—me missing you."

"Come here, you're cold," he said, shaking his head in disbelief. He took her in his arms again. "I happened to glance in and saw a woman who reminded me of you, but the sun was strong, and people were walking by, and I couldn't see. I was so sure my mind was playing tricks because you weren't in Paris. Only you were. Crazy."

"Unbelievable."

"So, what were you doing in Paris last weekend?"

Just say it. With him, there was no alternative to the truth.

"Octavia has a teacher, her mentor . . . a dominatrix, who holds this big annual event, like a retreat, for the people she's worked with over the years. She lives in a manor house outside Paris, on an incredible estate—it's like something from a movie—I wish you could have seen it. Anyway, Octavia invited me, and . . ."

Say it.

Here it was, the moment she would lose him. Her

sadness at the airport when she saw the newspaper head-lines returned, socking her in the belly once more.

Realizing she had been talking to the buttons on his shirt, she raised her gaze and firmly held his. "Octavia invited me, and I joined her. It was fantastic, profound." She put her palm on his chest, then quickly lifted it before he could reject her touch and move it away. "I know you don't understand . . ."

He surprised her by grabbing her hand. "Hey, hey, hey . . . shhh. I never want you to hesitate telling me *anything*. I need to share something with you, too—I want to explain." He held her wrist to keep her palm against his chest. "Me having issues with you and Octavia's was not because I didn't trust you, or because I have any issues with the life-style, or because I'm a possessive jerk with a big ego. I mean, I might be a jerk with a big ego, but that's a whole separate issue."

Even amid a serious conversation, one that could make or break them, he could make her laugh.

"Ever since our first night, I've tried to be conscious of your grief, your healing process. I understand it's not a linear thing, so I've tried to be careful with what I say to you, what I share with you, how much I ask of you. I've lost count of the number of times I wanted to hold you, spend the night, kiss you, touch you in ways I didn't think you would be ready for, so I didn't. I shoved all those wants aside, telling myself it was out of respect for you and to give you the space you need—and that was true.

"But I also didn't want to scare you away. I felt so lucky you picked me that night, that you landed in my lap. In a manner of speaking." His mouth quirked in a sweet half-smile as he realized the double entendre. "And I didn't want to risk doing or saying anything to ruin it. I tiptoed on eggshells. But if we're going to find a way forward, I need to tell you how I feel."

She started to voice her agreement, but he brought his index finger to her lips. *Shhh.*

Just like she had gently silenced him their first night, although so much had changed since then. "Don't say anything. Please." He replaced his index finger with his thumb and caressed her bottom lip. "You may not be ready to hear it, but I need to say it. I need you to know. I love you, Quinn. I'm in love with you."

His words drew the breath right out of her and, like lightning, he put his index finger back to her lips and pressed. "Don't say anything. Not now."

He rested his forehead at the top of hers, and she breathed in his sigh, felt his heart pounding under her hand.

"I hope that helps you understand why the club got under my skin—I felt like I was getting closer and closer to you and yet, by going there, you were part of something very separate from me, from us. It wasn't fair of me but—"

She rubbed his chest. "I'm sorry I hurt you. You're right, I wasn't ready. The day after you helped me move, after we kissed and spent the night, the feelings got to be too strong, too overwhelming. From the beginning, somehow, without words, without kissing, you knew my body, you knew *me*. Being so close petrified me. This is strange to say to you, possibly even hurtful, but I still miss him—I'm trying to live my life, but I miss him. And I couldn't risk being gutted like that again."

He held her tighter and swept his lips against her forehead, gave her the lightest kiss. "I know. It's not hurtful at all, and I'm so sorry." He was quiet for a moment, then added, "I understand if you're not ready, if you'll never be, I do."

"A relationship with you *terrifies* me." She closed her eyes and leaned against him.

"It scares me too, but I want to try." He held her close, his hand warm around the side of her head. "So, where does that leave us?"

"I'll be happier being terrified *with* you than without you."

They both laughed. It wasn't the most eloquent expression of commitment, but it was their reality.

The club was her reality as well.

She looked up into his eyes, pushed lightly against his chest to make space between them once more. "But please don't ask me not to go to Octavia's. It's becoming an important part of my life and she's a good friend."

"I won't ask that of you. Not sure exactly how I'll get my head around it, but I'll figure it out."

"*We'll* figure it out." Something sparked inside her; Jonathan with her at the club presented a universe of wonderfully erotic possibilities. "What if we go together sometime?"

He sighed again, his thumb grazing her cheek in a conciliatory way that told her he didn't want to let her down. "That's not a great idea right now—you know, the optics."

"Right. Of course. Your show." She smoothed the pleat of his shirt. His tuxedo shirt. "Wait, Leigh mentioned the awards were tonight. Did you win?"

He took her hand by the wrist, then pressed his palm flat against hers. "Sort of?"

Whatever that answer meant, he was hurt. "I'm sorry."

"It's okay—it crystallized things for me, so it's all good. I'll tell you about it another time, okay?" Heat blazed in his eyes as he traced a line down her throat with the pad of his thumb.

She lifted her chin to lengthen the trail he followed, relishing him touching her again. "Whenever you're ready." All she wanted right now was to get into bed and curl herself around him. Well, that wasn't *all* she wanted, but it would move them in the right direction.

She unbuttoned his shirt and slid it off him, and he tossed it over the chair with his jacket, stepped out of his pants and tight boxers, and threw those on the pile, too. "I just had an idea about the club," she blurted. "If you want to come with me, you could wear a mask."

She was picturing Maximillian. "There's at least one member who's always fully masked; I wouldn't recognize him outside the club if we bumped into each other."

The idea didn't thrill him. That was written plainly on his face. "I guess that's a possibility. But I've worn a mask for a long time, Quinn. Not sure I want to put on a real one now. But, hey, how about you get past the wedding next week and then we can figure things out? The club is important to you, so I'd like to be part of it if I can."

Relieved of his clothes, he turned back toward her and held her forearms, but he left some space between them. The sheer hunger in his eyes as his gaze traveled down and back up her naked body was rivaled by her own surging desire.

They had talked enough tonight.

She took his hand in hers and led him to the bed, pulling back the bright white summer duvet so they could climb in.

The light weight of the down comforter and the chill in the air, they were a reminder that summer was fleeting. She brought the duvet with her as she rolled on top of him, planting soft, light kisses down his neck and chest.

She caressed his torso, wove her fingers through the curls, traced and kissed a constellation of three birthmarks she hadn't noticed before.

She had been so lost in bleakness. She had needed; he had given. Now it was her turn to lavish attention on him, make him feel special and known.

She followed the path of salt and pepper curls downward, touching him again, working his length until he was fully hard. When she took him in her mouth, he held her head and exhaled her name in pleasure. But soon he softened, and she glanced up. "Tell me what you like."

Gently, with his hands on her jaw, he pulled her head away. "Hey. Come here."

She slid up to lie on her side next to him, but he guided her to her back, propping himself on his elbow beside her. She stroked his bicep. "You have to tell me what you like—I want you to. I'm not as good a mind reader as you are."

The skin around his eyes bunched as he smiled at the compliment. "It was perfect."

She slid her hand down to touch him, flaccid and small. "It couldn't have been that perfect."

"Quinn." He moved her hand away, abruptly serious. The rebuff stung. "I stopped you because I want to make sure you're ready. To make love. That's the only way I want us to be together tonight, and I don't want you to be sorry later or regret that it was too soon."

Her eyes met the intensity of his, and she shook her head to underscore what she was about to say. "Jonathan, I will not be sorry."

He placed his palm on her chest, as if he wanted the words to penetrate. "I know this isn't how you saw your life unfolding. I know you never expected to be with another man. You never expected to have to pick up the pieces and start over. I know, I do."

He moved his hand higher, cupped her jaw and cheek, then leaned down and kissed her forehead. "So I understand if you're not ready to make love. We can wait as long as you need."

His words, his tenderness, him. Her eyes teared up at the bitter sweetness of it. So often she was reminded of the void Harris left, all the flashes of longing and memory. But maybe the contours of that void were changing, shifting to create space for the rare gift of a second chance.

She put her hand over his while he touched her face. "I am ready. With you, I'm ready."

The twinkle returned to his eye when he smiled. He kissed the tip of her nose. "I have one more condition."

"Oh, really?" she teased. "What is it?"

"Tonight, no toys, no games, no blindfold, no pain. Nothing but you and me. Nothing between us. I want all of you with me tonight."

She grazed his cheek with her thumb, traced his brow and the curve of the bone beneath his eye. "You have all of me tonight." Her smile merged with his kiss as she pulled his body against hers, warm and strong. And hard. "Now, what are you waiting for?"

17

ERASED OF ALL RATIONAL
THOUGHT

He wanted to say they should go slow, that they had all night to draw this out. But the way she kidded about the urgency and the genuine desire he heard in her voice, slow took a fast dive out the window.

"I'm going to try for this not to be over in three minutes," he muttered, his lips nearing her breast, "but I make no promises."

"You are such a romantic." Her back arched, and he couldn't tell whether it was because she laughed, or because his mouth found her nipple. He kept it there, laving and tasting, getting reacquainted with her body.

Slowly, he slid his hand down her smooth belly. She gasped and held his head to her breast as he continued his journey.

She had told him she was ready emotionally; her wetness told him she was ready physically. Careful not to rest all his weight on her, he moved over her and she reached to kiss him, her big brown eyes right there with him like he asked, like she promised, her legs wrapping around his, then higher, hooking onto his hips.

As their lips parted for each other, as they savored and explored, while he stroked and held the side of her face, he slid inside her. The air of her rhythmic moans tickled the roof of his mouth as she took him in.

She held him close, fingertips pressed into his back as he thrust slow and deep without leaving her body. If they didn't stop kissing, he was going to lose all self-control, so he paused and playfully nipped her lower lip before burying his face in her neck.

99 . . . 98 . . . 97 . . .

Like her hair, her skin held the faintest scent of raspberry that erased his mind of any rational thought.

Except one.

It wouldn't matter if she went to the club or what he did with his career or anything else he would be challenged to figure out in the future because with her he was himself, and he was home.

THE HEAT and weight of his body pressed her against the bed, every part of him holding her close and in place, and yet the undulating movement of their bodies gave her the sensation of floating.

That's how it was with him, that's how it had been from their very first night. Boundaries blurred. Rough, tender. Restraint, freedom. Isolation, connection.

Love, risk.

She brought his head up from her neck so she could look at him, touch his face, kiss him again.

The molten core of her body drew him deeper, bringing

them both to the edge of exquisite pleasure. No, she didn't need to protect her heart from him, she needed to share it with him. And as his tongue, his lips, his breath entwined with hers, as they let themselves slip over the edge together, she did.

AUTHOR'S NOTE

Thank you for reading *Secretly*! It feels like a lot happens in this moment in Quinn and Jonathan's relationship. Come to think of it, a lot happens in many other relationships in the story, too—in Quinn's friendship with Octavia, between Jonathan and Delphine, and between Octavia and Madame Manon.

Usually when I write, I work from an outline. Not always the most detailed outline (although sometimes it is), but an outline, nonetheless. But in this case, the characters had their own ideas, and they drove the story in ways I hadn't expected. Octavia inviting Quinn to Paris, the whole world of Manon's château, Jonathan's decision about his job (being purposely vague here in case, like me, you read authors' notes before the book)—I had not initially seen those coming. Nearly every character in this story surprised me in some way.

Possibly the next best job after being a travel show host like Jonathan is being a writer. But writing about Paris partially during the COVID-19 pandemic meant I was not taking a research trip. The routes Quinn, Jonathan, and

Delphine walk, the stationery store, the restaurant, the café —they're all fictional, as is the generic convention center that hosts the travel expo. So, don't plan your trip to Paris around the places in this story. ;)

While revising the manuscript, I thought about cutting the scene in Montmartre where the mime sketches Quinn and Jonathan individually—when they each think they've seen the other but tell themselves that's impossible. But ultimately I chose to keep it, since its theme quietly echoes throughout the book—the idea that, sometimes, limitations we perceive are self-imposed.

If you'd like to share more of Quinn and Jonathan's and other characters' journeys, including a startling discovery that threatens to destroy *many* relationships, you'll want to read *Entirely* next. (The Transformation series is best read in order.)

For advance notice of new books and bonus content, please visit talyablaine.com and sign up for my email list. This is the best way to stay in touch.

At my site, you'll also find a Reader and Book Club Guide for *Secretly* as well as the other books.

Did you enjoy *Secretly*? I'd be thrilled if you'd leave a review on your favorite review site, such as Goodreads and BookBub, and your preferred retailer website.

Thank you! Your support means the world.

XO,
Talya

ABOUT THE AUTHOR

Talya Blaine specializes in writing older characters, including strong heroines and sexy, "beta" heroes, and in exploring how relationships change with time. *Secretly* is her second romance novel, a book *Publishers Weekly* Book-Life Prize reviewers called *"hot and deliciously steamy."*

When she's not working at her day job in marketing, she loves to write steamy romances, read, and blog; hike with her border collie; and spend time with Mr. Blaine, her real-life romance hero.

To be notified of new books and exclusive offers for subscribers, join her email list at talyablaine.com.

BB bookbub.com/authors/talya-blaine

g goodreads.com/talyablaine

ALSO BY TALYA BLAINE

Transformation Series

Silently (Book 1)

"This is a unique work with fascinating characters, drawn together as they individually recover from profound loss." -The BookLife Prize

Secretly (Book 2)

"Blaine excels at crafting a plausible plot and ratcheting up the heat and chemistry..."

"Hot and deliciously steamy..." -The BookLife Prize

Entirely (Book 3)

"Blaine continues the Transformation series with this third installment, spilling over with steamy bedroom scenes..."

"...the deep interplay between the two main characters adds a special intimacy to the novel." -The BookLife Prize